# Tales of a Maltese Village

## Part Two

# arry Goes to the Dogs

# Roy Martin

# Tales of a Maltese Village

Part Two

## Harry goes to the Dogs

Roy Martin

This book is the work of fiction. People, places, events and situations are the product of the Author's imagination. Any resemblance to actual persons living or dead or historical events is purely coincidental.

No part of this book may be reproduced, stored in a retrieval system or transmitted by any means without the written permission of the author.

# The Author

The author Roy Martin, was born in Kent in England six months before the second World War broke out. His mother insists there was no connection!  Having been educated at Borden Grammar School in Sittingbourne, he joined the RAF in 1958 and was trained as a photographer.

Most of his RAF career was spent in Malta where he met and married his Maltese sweetheart, Lucy. They were married in the church at Ħal-Luqa in 1963 and returned to Kent where Roy continued his photographic interest in the retail trade. Roy and Lucy have four children, eight grand children and six great grand children.

After a life time spent in the photographic trade Roy has now retired to his beloved island of Malta and lives in the same village that is the subject of his book.

Dedicated to my ever patient wife Lucy and our children Yvonne, Sarah, Tania and Andrei, and to all my friends and family in Malta.

# The Dream becomes reality.

"If there is one thing I can't stand it is the sight of a plate with a half eaten sausage roll on it" complained George.

"*Heqq*! What brought that on?" exclaimed Harry "Here we are enjoying a quiet pint and you come out with an earth shattering statement like that!"

"Well, it's true. I cannot stand waste. Leaving a sausage roll is a symbol of an uncaring selfish attitude to life" continued George, waving his finger in the air "There are thousands in this world who would give anything for a sausage roll."

"Including Fart no doubt" added Aris.

Fart, Bungalow's faithful dog raised an ear at the mention of a sausage roll.

"George, if this is the start of one of your rants then I for one am out of here" said Harry.

"See. That is the trouble. When faced with a serious issue, you all back away and refuse to face up to it. What hope is there for the world if we all do that?" said George.

"Because there is no point in beating yourself up over something that you can't do anything about" reasoned Harry "Anyway, there is a greater sight that I cannot stand and we can do something about it."

"And that is?" asked George.

"The sight of three empty beer glasses! Your round I believe George" said Harry.

"Nice one Harry" chuckled Aris.

"OK I know when I am beaten. Ho set them up. One Cisk, one Hop Leaf and one Blue label, *jekk jogħġbok.*" George knew when to pull back.

"One Cisk, one Hop Reaf and one Brue Raboo coming up" said Ho. As the dutiful and caring landlord of the Ho Chi Do Chi Bar, Ho was careful never to take sides. His experience of working his own bar in Hong Kong had long ago taught him the art of bar room diplomacy.

"And I tell you something else that annoys me" George was getting into his stride "Table cloths!"

"Table cloths!" scoffed Aris "The man's lost it! Why would anyone complain about table cloths?"

"Table cloths in a bar" insisted George "It isn't right. No disrespect to Do of course. She has done a grand job but a bar is a bar not a cafe or snack bar. Bare tables, bare floor boards. That is a bar."

"You're still living in the past George" said Harry "Times have moved on. You are being left behind."

"Well that's another thing" no stopping George now "Why do women want to cover small tables and coffee tables with cloths and doilies. Especially crocheted ones."

"Don't let Carmena hear him" laughed Pawlu "She will have sixty fits."

"What is the point of spending lots of money on a magnificent oak or walnut table and then hiding it under a piece of crochet?" continued George "You should know that Pawlu, being a carpenter."

"Hey, don't drag me into it" protested Pawlu "Live and let live I say. Can't we change the subject?"

"Good idea. So, how are things going with the kennels, Harry?" asked George changing the subject.

"Don't ask" replied Harry "Sometimes I wish I had never started. I think I am out of my depth."

"Oh come on. This was your dream. Surely you're not getting cold feet."

"No, it's not that" said Harry "I have some wonderful help from lots of people but I guess I am not cut out to be a business man. I am getting too old."

"Then you must delegate the work to others. That's what the big boys do" said George.

"If truth be known it is Andrew the Mayor who has done all the work. He is the one who got planning permission and has raised extra funds to complete the project. I have to say he has been magnificent" said Harry.

"Then why the doubts?" asked Aris.

"You're right. I should be more positive. I must trust in my dream and enjoy the moment" said Harry resigning himself to his fate.

"I'll drink to that" said George raising his glass.

It was now some ten years since Harry's sister Joan had brought the news of their inheritance. Harry had not seen his sister in years. She lived in Scotland and he lived in Malta. But with the death of their Aunt Alice in Birkenhead and the settlement of her estate, the siblings heard that they had inherited over a million pounds between them. After the initial shock, Harry began to think what he would do with the windfall. Money had never really featured in Harry's life. He had never had any! He had always been content to jog along quietly. As long as he had a roof over his head, food on the table and a few glasses of his favourite Blue Label, he was happy.

Needless to say the patrons of Ho's bar were only too ready to give him advice on how to spend his inheritance and it was during one of their conversations that Harry hit upon the idea of breeding greyhounds and setting up a dog racing stadium in Malta. By a stroke of luck Andrew the Mayor of Ħal-Luqa was in the bar that night and had overheard the discussion. Not one to miss an opportunity he joined in. The Mayor was quick to realise that the introduction of greyhound racing to the island could be a big vote winner and would be very popular with the population. It would generate many jobs especially in the catering trade at which the Maltese excelled. Andrew was very well connected and it was not long before wheels were turning.

Over the next ten years, planning permission was granted for the stadium to be built at Ta Qali. The land at the old airfield was prepared and the new stadium was being built. Although it had been Harry's idea to build at the Marsa race course, the golfers had put a stop to it even though they had been promised a state of the art golf course between Pembroke and Baħar Iċ–Ċaqq. Maltese do not like change. In the event Ta Qali would prove to be a better choice. So everyone was happy.

Apart from the money put up by Harry and Joan, the government allocated funds and more money was granted through the EU. Mayor Andrew had been very busy. The project had attracted much interest from entrepreneurs in Germany and England and several had committed to setting up their own racing kennels on the island.

All Harry had to do was sit back and let it happen. Well, almost. His part in all of the action was to set up his own kennels. It was Harry's dream to own his own dogs and race them at the new stadium. But first he had to locate some dogs that he could start breeding. Then he needed somewhere to set up his kennels.

Locating the dogs was his first problem. He had no idea what to look for nor where to look. In fact if t was all left to him he could easily be sold a pup! Once again Harry had a stroke of luck. It appeared that Idaho Joe had been involved in some dog racing in Australia – albeit illegal – and professed to know a good dog when he saw one. It was also the case that Angus who was Joan's husband had some knowledge of greyhounds. So it was decided that Joe would go to the UK to meet up with Angus and between them they would buy a dog and a bitch and have them flown to Malta for Harry to set up his kennels and hopefully start his own line of racing dogs.

"Come with me, Harry" said Idaho "It is only a couple of hours to England. You can help us find the dogs."

"I'd rather not, thanks Joe. I wouldn't know what to look for and I hate flying anyway."

 "Didn't know you hated flying Harry" said Joe "Nothing to it nowadays. Safest means of travel in fact."

"I don't know about that. As Michael Flanders said 'If God had intended us to fly he would not have given us the railways'. All I can say is I would fly if they left the doors open. I hate being shut in."

"Fair enough" said Joe "You can leave it to me and Angus. We will do our best for you Harry."

"I know you will. And thank you. You know I appreciate it" said a relieved Harry.

   And so it was that Idaho Joe met up with Angus in the UK and after visiting many kennels they bought a fine dog from a kennels in Catford and a magnificent bitch from a kennels in Manchester. Their pedigrees were immaculate. The registered name of the dog was 'Lord Nodagan'.

"What sort of name is that?" laughed Angus.

Apparently when the dog was pup he had a tendency to do his business wherever and whenever he chose and the owner on finding his little 'presents' would say "Oh Lord. Not again." Hence 'Lord Nodagan'. The bitch was named 'Her Ladyship' because of her regal demeanour.

Both dogs had finished their racing lives and were fit, healthy and strong.  Their offspring would surely be winners. All the paperwork was completed and the dogs were despatched to Malta for their new lives.

Meanwhile Harry had been busy finding a suitable site for his kennels. Bungalow's father owned some land near Dingli cliffs which he no longer farmed and he was happy to rent it out to Harry. The farm buildings themselves had been used to house and breed goats so it was no major task to convert them into kennels. The area was also protected by a seven foot high stone wall making it secure from predators and nosey passersby. Harry also knew that greyhounds could jump very high so the high walls were a neccessity.

The dogs had to be cleared from quarantine, which would normally take around six months but with a little of who you know and other incentives that nobody talked about the delay was reduced to a couple of weeks–this was Malta after all. Harry, with the assistance of his pals from the Ho Chi Do Chi Bar soon had them settled in. It was now a matter of waiting for what they hoped would be the inevitable.

One thing that did concern Harry was the security and running of the site. It was OK to have the dogs nicely ensconced in their quarters but they would need to be regularly fed and exercised. Although greyhounds are naturally lazy animals they would still need walking twice a day for about twenty minutes. Always on a leash of course as a greyhound will chase anything that moves and considering they can reach speeds in excess of forty miles an hour, Idaho would not have stood a chance catching them. Forasmuch as Idaho Joe was a great help in looking after the dogs, he was getting on a bit and it clearly needed a younger man to do the job. The obvious choice was Bungalow. He did not earn a lot of money on the bins and he was usually finished work by midday. He readily accepted the challenge.

"Do I get a uniform?" he asked.

"Of course" said Harry. "You will be the official security guard." Bungalow was delighted.

"And will Fart be my guard dog?" he asked

"I see no reason why not" replied Harry.

Bungalow and Fart were going up in the World. Not only did Fart have his own Villa, *Il-Kelb Tas-Siġġiewi,* but he was now the official guard dog at the Harry Barber Kennels. Pawlu had built the Villa for Fart after the patrons of the Ho Chi Do Chi Bar decided they could no longer put up with the regular and severely pungent emissions from Fart's rear end especially after a meal of sausage rolls and cauliflower. The kennel that Pawlu had built now stood outside the entrance to the bar and Fart loved it.

Harry was starting to feel pleased with himself. At last things were falling into place. The kennels were ready, the dogs had arrived, he had his security guard, the stadium was well advanced and all the legal arrangements had been settled.  All that remained was for Lord Nodagan and Her Ladyship to perform, the pups to arrive and after about a year, training could start.

It would be down to Angus and Idaho to organise the training schedules when the pups were old enough. Angus had moved to Malta with his wife Joan when he retired from his job as a coach driver taking tourists around Europe. His journeys had taken him to many European countries and he had picked up a good knowledge of European languages. The Maltese language was beyond him!

"It is the most difficult language I have ever come across" he remarked "A five year old can pick it up but for me it is impossible."

"Don't worry Angus. Most Maltese know English and the ones that don't can always make themselves understood" explained Harry "Take Salvu,  Pawlu's father. He once wanted to explain to me about a 'colander'. I had no idea what he was trying to say. Then he said 'Spaghetti hello. Water bye bye'. I knew exactly what he meant. No problem."

"Och aye" said Angus "I'll be OK. Anyway, it is up to the dogs now. I'm looking forward to my new job as a dog trrainer".

"And I am sure you will do a grand job" said Harry "Here, have another sausage roll while you finish your whisky."

"I shouldn't really" said Angus "I am supposed to be on a diet. Don't tell Joan" he said biting off half of the roll.

Ho rang the bar bell to remind the patrons that the day was over and it was time to go home and have a good rest. As they left the bar George saw the remains of Angus's sausage roll on the plate.

"See what I mean" he ranted "My words mean nothing. Another half sausage bound for the dust bin. What a waste of good food!"

"All right George, don't start" said Harry "If it offends you, give it to Fart. It will be gratefully received and faithfully devoured."

# The Confession.

The large articulated lorry that had pulled up in the square had caught Harry's eye. It was loaded with about a dozen iron girders about twenty feet in length. What were they going to do with them? Was the church roof about to fall down? Were they going to build an extension? His curiosity was matched by several of the villagers who had also gathered to see what was going on. Earlier that morning notices had been pinned on all the doors of the church advising parishioners not to enter. This was serious stuff. The church was never closed to anyone! Something big must be going on.

The great doors at the entrance to the church were opened and a small mobile fork lift entered. Several men then proceeded to move the girders from the lorry onto the fork lift and into the church.

There was nothing else for it. Someone had to find old Guisseppa. She knew everything about everything and everyone. If anyone knew what was happening it would be her. Harry could tell from the noise coming from the band club that she had been found. He casually strolled over, not wishing to appear too interested.

It was then that he noticed Pawlu talking to the Kappillan. *"Bonġu Pawlu, Bonġu Kappillan, Kif Int?"* said Harry using almost his full vocabulary of Maltese "What is going on in the church? Do you know?"

"Ah yes" answered the priest "Nice to see you Harry. They are starting on the restoration of the cupola. It will be redecorated with all the gold facia renovated. Big job. Will take some time I expect."

"Wow. What are the girders for?" asked Harry.

"They will be the support for a platform for the workmen to stand on. They will be removed when they finish."

"How long will that take" asked Pawlu.

"A year or so I expect. Longer if they run out of money."

Harry was curious to see inside.

"Is it OK to watch while they put the girders in place?" he asked.

"Well strictly speaking, no. It is against health and safety but if you come with me through the sacristy you will be able to watch from a distance."

Harry was curious to see what was going on. He followed the Kappillan who directed him to a corner of the church where he had a good view.

The fork lift had a long cantilever arm which raised the girders up to the top of the great pillars of the church and rested them on the overhangs. Harry thought it looked quite precarious. But then many things in the building trade struck Harry as precarious – even dangerous. Liberties were always being taken sometimes with disastrous consequences but most of the time they worked.

It was not long before the criss-cross of girders was complete and the bright yellow interlocking planks had been placed in position to form a working platform. Harry was impressed. A tarpaulin screen had also been ra sed that would prevent parishioners from seeing the work that would be going on. Years ago Harry remembered going to Gozo where they were building the church of Ta Pinu. He recalled that the Italian stonemasons had been working their art carving the roof in the most intricate and ornate fashion. But as soon as strangers entered the church area they would stop work. The would not resume work until the visitors had left.The secrets of their trade had to be preserved.

With the workmen gone and the church restored to a respectful peace and silence, Harry decided to sit a while and enjoy the solitude of the moment. Harry was not a churchgoer but he had a great respect for the church, for the clergy and for churchgoers. Besides, as Mass was spoken in Maltese he had no idea what was being said! At least that was his excuse. Today though he felt he wanted to dally awhile. It was probably the closest he would come to actually attending a Mass. But that was OK.
Harry sat in one of the alcoves and leant against the ornately carved wooden backrest.

*"Fl–isem Tal-Missier u Ta 'l–ibnu u ta l–Ispirtu s-Santu."*

A voice came from behind the wooden backrest.

"Eh?" said Harry.

"Make your confession my son" said the voice.

"Confession!" exclaimed Harry "Er. No, no there is a mistake. I was just taking a rest. Sorry."

"It is all right. Not to worry. Stay awhile. Let's chat. Have you not been to confession before?" the voice asked.

"Well yes. A long time ago."

"How Long?"

"I can't remember– maybe when I was a boy."

"A boy!" remarked the voice "Now I am guessing that that was a very long time ago."

"Well yes it was. Fifty years probably."

"And you are a Catholic and you have not been to confession for fifty years! How can that be?" asked the voice.

"It sounds terrible doesn't it?" admitted Harry "I just never got round to it really. But then I never really understood it either. I never felt the need."

"How often have I heard that!" mumbled the voice.

"No honestly, I would not know what to say. I mean I lead a fairly good life. I have not committed any crimes or cheated any one. What is there to say?"

"But that is the point, you do not have to wait until you murder someone before you come to confession."

Harry sensed the voice was smiling.

"Confession is not there just to get you off the hook for criminal activity, you know."

"Well I must confess that I have thought of murdering Fart the dog when he has dropped one" mused Harry.

"And who hasn't" chuckled the voice.

"Well yes, I think I understand that but what else is there to confess?" said a confused Harry.

"All confession does is to ask you to take few moments of your time to stop, step back and take a look at yourself. Examine what you have done over the last week. Have you been angry with someone? Could you have helped someone rather than step back because it was too much trouble? Have you used bad language? Have you been disrespectful?" asked the voice "I know these may seem trivial but they are all part of your character. They are all part of making you a better person. All confession does is to concentrate the mind. We are all too busy with our day to day chores to examine ourselves. Too wrapped up in the modern hurly burly of life to see where we are going astray."

"Maybe you're right" thought Harry.

"It is good to take a couple of minutes to analyse what you have been doing, to refresh your soul. And who better than a priest to listen to you. You know that he will never repeat what you say and will never think worse of you, provided you promise to do better of course."

"Ok but I have fifty years to confess for. Where do I start? You will be here all day if I get going."

"The fact you are here is a start. Think over what we have said and maybe you will come next time on purpose– not because you accidently sat in the confessional chair."

Harry was beginning to like this priest. He reminded him of the priest at his church when he was a boy. The 'Lardy' Priest as they used to call him. He was from Dublin and he used to say *"The Lard be wit choo".*

"You know Father, I might just do that" Harry laughed "And I promise I will not strangle Fart the dog next time he pollutes the atmosphere. I reckon that dog has contributed more to global warming than any amount of petrol fumes."

It was the priests turn to laugh.

"No, but I will kill Bungalow for feeding him rotten cauliflower instead." The priest clearly knew his parish.

The solemnity of the church was broken by the laughter of the two men.

# A Bolt out of the blue.

Peace. Quiet. Tranquillity. In the hectic, chaotic, and stress laden world that we live in, the opportunity to find a safe haven, a private place, anywhere where we can be alone with our thoughts is something that we all aspire to. None the least Harry Barber. Harry had always led a quiet life. He avoided confrontation and in spite of his responsible rank in the Royal Navy he hated making decisions.  His life in Ħal-Luqa had been ideal. He had his daily routine based on the discipline learned from the close quarters of the various ships he had sailed in. His trusted housekeeper Lucia had kept him on the straight and narrow and ensured that he ate well and kept himself and his house clean. He had no responsibilities and had a circle of good friends whose company he enjoyed and treasured. A glass of beer, lively conversation and good friends. What more could a man ask for!

But ever since Harry had embarked on his project to run his own kennels and with his involvement in the new greyhound stadium at Ta Qali, life had been far from peaceful. He was beginning to regret having got involved. So it was that whenever he sought some isolation and privacy where he could get his thoughts together he would go to the cliffs at Dingli and sit outside the St. Mary Magdalene chapel.

*Il-Kappella Ta'Santa Marija Maddalena* has stood defiantly, proudly and totally isolated on the edge of the cliffs since 1646 although records indicate there was an altar there some two hundred years earlier. The chapel is known locally as *Il-Kappella Tal-Irdum* – the Chapel of the Cliffs. The feast is held on the 22nd July but many villagers also visit on Passion Sunday.

Being one of the highest and most barren points of the Maltese islands, the cliffs can be relied upon to be free from pollution thanks to the constant breeze which on occasions can suddenly turn into a raging gale.

It was the rawness of the garrigue that appealed to Harry. The bland greyness of the limestone rock face deceived the traveller into believing there was nothing of interest here but the more discerning viewer would soon begin to find some of the most beautiful flowers and plants on God's earth.

The lack of rain for most of the year and the intense and unrelenting heat of summer made one wonder how anything could survive in this environment. But when the rains did come

and winter settled in, the plants that had been lying dormant and
hiding from the scorching sun would explode into a glorious
panorama of colour. The small flowers were perfectly formed
being free from the ravaging effects of pollution. Vistas of pure
purple Mediterranean Thyme, Maltese Rock Centaury – the
national flower of Malta, Yellow Kidney Vetch, Hoary Rock Rose,
Hare's tail grass, Wild Artichoke, Yellow Throated Crocus and
beautiful wild Antirrhinums growing out of the stone walls were a
joy to behold.

As Harry sat outside the chapel looking out to sea at the island
of Filfla, lost in his own thoughts and as close to nature as he
could be, it began to rain. Heavy rain clouds were approaching
from the North. There was no shelter but Harry did not care. He
welcomed the life–giving drops of rain knowing how important
they were to the dormant life of the cliffs. The lizards, the
constant and ever vigilant guardians of the garrigue darted for
cover. A sure sign that bad weather was approaching.

It was December so storms were to be expected. As Harry
surveyed the skies he realised that he was in for a major storm.
He could hear the rumble of thunder which rolled around the
island. The storm had already convulsed Gozo and Komino and
was steadily spreading its blanket of torrential rain across the
island. The black thunder clouds now obliterated the sun and the
garrigue took on a menacing face. As the intensity of the storm
increased so the torrents of rain formed new rivers in the road
and began cascading down the cliffs doing their best to drag the
soil with them into the ever demanding sea. The local farmers

had built many retaining walls to protect their land from the rains but sometimes nature would win, breaking through the stones and dragging them seawards.

Harry decided to make for his treasured Chevrolet Impala as the first flash of lightning lit up the morning sky. The safest place in such a violent storm was a car. No sooner had Harry closed the door of the Chevvy than a ferocious streak of lightning struck the chapel causing much damage to the ancient building – and not for the first time! Harry had just made it in time otherwise he would have been fried by the lightning strike. It was the 10th December 2014 and Harry resolved to make this date a special one in his calendar. So much for peace and quiet.

Harry chuckled to himself. He had come to Dingli to escape the pressures of his life in the village and had walked straight into one the most violent storms he had ever experienced.

Perhaps it was a sign. Maybe someone was telling him that his worries were nothing compared to the power of nature.  There were other things to worry about – like all that nature throws at you and that you can do nothing about. Yes, that was it. Nothing really mattered. Accept what fate has thrown at you and make the best of it. Let it happen and just enjoy it. That was what was needed. Just as the pelting rain and dark clouds meant he could hardly see his hand in front of his face so the flashes of lightning had opened his eyes to new vista. That is when it struck him. He would call his two best dogs, Thunder and Lightning.

Suddenly all Harry's woes had vanished. The clouds of dismay had cleared and although the storm still raged under a blackened sky, all Harry could see was a blue horizon. His doubts had washed away down the rivers that gushed through the garrigue to the sea below.

He knew now what he had to do. His kennels were real. His dogs had an identity. He had the unstinting support of the villagers of Ħal-Luqa. What could possibly go wrong!

Harry pressed the starter of his trusty Chevrolet Impala and as the engine burst into life as it had done for the last sixty years, he headed for the farm where Pawlu was putting the finishing touches to the kennels.

"Hey Pawlu" greeted Harry "How's it going?"

"*Tajjeb*" replied Pawlu with a big smile. "Glad to see the back of that storm though."

 "The kennels are looking magnificent" observed Harry "I think I might move in myself."

Pawlu was never happier than when he was working with wood. Any excuse to make something and he was your man. "*Grazzi*" said Pawlu "I think the dogs are happy here. That is the main thing."

"Pawlu, I was thinking about the names for the puppies when they are born and it came to me as the lightning struck up on the cliffs. I have decided that the two best puppies from our first litter will be named Thunder and Lightning. What do you think?"

"I suppose this storm had nothing to do with naming them, did it?" laughed Pawlu. Harry nodded. "Great names. Let's hope the dogs are as formidable as that storm."

The storm had not disturbed the dogs at all. Greyhounds are quite lazy creatures in fact and spend much of their time lying down. It is only when they see something move that they take off. They also like to jump. That is one reason why Pawlu had erected a high fence around the compound. The other was to keep out inquisitive strangers.

"I'm going back to the village now Pawlu. Would you like a lift?" asked Harry.

"No, it is OK. I have my trusty old RAF bike with me and it's stopped raining now and anyway I don't want to leave the dogs until Bung and Fart get here" replied Pawlu "I guess he missed his bus again."

"Yes. I must do something about that. Maybe get him some driving lessons."

"Or a bike" suggested Pawlu.

"Well maybe but I can't see Fart running behind him for far" Harry chuckled at the thought. As far as Fart was concerned exercise was a totally alien concept. His only activities were eating and sleeping.

As they spoke so Bungalow with his faithful dog Fart appeared running up the steep road to the farm.

"Sorry I'm late Mr Harry. The bus was late arriving" Bung explained.

"No worry Bung old chap" said Harry "You are here now that's the main thing. Bung I was thinking. So you won't have to rely on the buses, what do you think about getting some driving lessons? I'll pay of course. Are you up for it?"

"Yes sir. I would like very much" answered Bungalow "Thank you Mr Harry. Thank you very much" Bungalow was delighted.

He really was going up in the world. He may be a dust bin man in the mornings but he was also head security guard at the Harry Barber kennels with his own uniform, a guard dog, a walkie talkie and a mobile phone. Now he would have a driving licence as well. "Leave it to me" said Harry as he bade farewell to his pals. All in all Harry was well pleased with himself.

For what had started out as dismal day for him, he was now full of the joys of spring. The storm that had moved away from the island had cleared not only the dusty roads and limestone cliffs but had concentrated Harry's mind. Just as the storm abated and the weak winter sun warmed up the garrigue to encourage the beautiful flowers that lived there to open their arms in thanks for their much needed drink, so Harry had a new dawning. He now had a mission. A new determination to make things work. Just as St Paul had had his moment on the road to Damascus so Harry had his on the cliffs of Dingli. This was his Dingli moment.

He couldn't wait to get back to Ħal-Luqa to enjoy a drink with his pals. All he had to do now was arrange for Bung's driving lessons and wait for Lord Nodagan and Her Ladyship to produce their first litter.

An invigorated Harry drove a little faster than normal back through the streets of Buskett, Żebbuġ and Qormi to his home in Ħal-Luqa. He had to tell his pals at the Ho Chi Do Chi Bar about his new found motivation.

"Hi Ho" he said as he entered the bar "Where is everyone? It is quarter to seven and no George, no Aris. Never happened before. What's up?"

"All OK Mr Hally" said Ho " Evyone in church. The storm has damaged the church loof. They are creaning up mess."

"I better get over there and lend a hand" Harry made straight for the church.

"Hi George. What has happened? Boy what a mess" said Harry stepping over debris from the roof.

"Hi Harry" replied George "Yeah, bit of a catastrophe isn't it?"

"That was some storm Harry" Aris joined in "It looks like the wind gusted through the opening where the roof supports are and lifted the tarpaulin like a ship's sail. It took off and pulled some of the roof with it."

The work around the cupola had already been delayed mainly due to lack of funds but in the last few months great progress had been made. This was a bitter blow. Although none of the gold restoration work had been harmed the facings of some of the pillars had been destroyed. There was no lack of help as the villagers all lent their hands to clearing up the debris. The Kappillan was in the heart of it.

"So sorry to see this, Father" said Harry.

"These things happen, Harry" said the priest philosophically. "No-one can argue with the forces of nature. We have to get on with life and accept what is thrown at us with good faith. Mass will be delayed by about two hours and then back to normal."

"You're a good man Father. The village is lucky to have you" said Harry.

"No Harry. These are the good men. They have dropped everything to come to the aid of the church. They are the ones you should thank" the priest smiled with gratitude.

"Well Father I can tell you that you are not the only one in trouble because of the storm" said Harry.

"Oh! Why so?" asked the Father.

"Lightning struck the chapel of St Mary Magdalene at Dingli" he explained "Took most of the roof off."

"Oh dear. That's bad. No one hurt I hope."

"No. No one there actually, except me, but I was safe" said Harry.

"What were you doing up there? Are you crazy? Especially with such a big storm brewing?" asked George.

"Come to the bar and I'll tell you" replied Harry.

   As the clearing up was just about finished and given the large number of helpers, the lads decided they were not needed and reverted to Ho's bar.

"So what's it all about?" asked Aris once the drinks had been poured and the three had sat down.

"Well" said Harry "You know I've been a bit down these last few weeks. You know worried that I had taken on too much."

"Yeah. A right blooming misery at times" remarked George.

"Ok, Ok don't rub it in" continued Harry "Well I went up to Dingli to try to clear my mind."

"And did you" asked Aris.

 "Yes" replied Harry "I think I did."

"Go on then what happened?" asked George.

"As I was sitting with all the troubles of the world on my shoulders, the storm broke and there was a blinding flash. The chapel had been struck with a terrifying streak of lightning yet it still stood, strong as ever, defiantly withstanding everything the Gods had to throw at it. If the chapel could withstand the most incredible power of the storm then what was I worried about? My problems were infinitely small in comparison.  In that moment I realised that nothing mattered."

"Er, you've lost me" said George.

"No it's true. Nothing really matters. There are things in life, events, actions, you know things that you can do nothing about. Out of your control. So what is the point of worrying about them?"

"Well, yeah. I go along with that. Exactly what I was saying about half eaten sausage rolls. But what is that to do with you and your misery" asked George.

"Don't you see? All the time I have been working myself up about the kennels and the stadium when really it is all happening anyway. I can't stop it even if I wanted to. The ball is rolling and others are keeping it going" continued Harry "I know I started it but others will finish it. I should be standing back and enjoying it. So that is what I will do."

"Well, I will drink to that" said George not really convinced "Another round over here please, Ho."

"And there is another thing" said Harry.

"Don't tell me you have seen the light as well. I saw you very chummy with the priest" said George cynically.

"Almost" laughed Harry "No, I have decided on the names of my two best dogs when Her Ladyship produces her litter."

"Go on" said Aris.

"They will be named Thunder and Lightning" said Harry.

"Very appropriate. No doubt the storm had something to do with it" said Aris "I will drink to that. Gentlemen, here's to Thunder and Lightning. May they 'reign' supreme at the race track."

"Very funny" George smiled "But there's a long way to go yet. Her Ladyship is not even pregnant! Someone needs to have a word with Lord Nodagan. Time for him to perform I think."

"Give them a chance George" said Angus who had just joined the party "They have only just got to know each other. Can't rush these things, ye ken."

"You're right Angus" said Harry "It will happen in due course I guess. But once the pups are here how long before we can race them?"

"Well, we canna start trraining until they are about a year old and then they should be having their first rrace at arround eighteen months. So we have plenty of time yet" answered Angus.

"It will probably take that long to get the stadium sorted" added Aris.

The planning permission for the stadium had been approved thanks to the unstinting work and persuasive skills of Andrew the Mayor. His extensive contacts in government and abroad had attracted considerable interest and the project was well under way. It was now some ten years since Harry had come up with the idea and in that time the land had been procured, the stadium built, the track laid and all the operating infrastructure had been put in place. It was now a matter of sorting out the staff, the administration, the catering and the security. All these matters were in the Mayors domain. Harry kept out of it.

It was approaching closing time and the patrons of the Ho Chi Do Chi bar were drifting home.

"Last round" called George "Then off up the wooden hills to Bedfordshire."

The telephone at the back of the bar rang.

"One moment" said Ho. "I answer phone."

Ho took the call and having replaced the receiver, came rushing over to Harry, clearly distressed.

"Mr Hally, that was Bungarow. He say that he has heard strange noise and thinks someone is trying to blake in at kennel. He want you go there."

"Call him back and tell him I am on my way" said a concerned Harry.

"I'll come with you" said George.

They jumped into Harry's Chevvy and set off from the village not knowing what they would find in Dingli. The day was not yet over.

# Roger and Out

"What time is it?" asked Harry as he sped up the steep hill towards Rabat.

"Just after eleven" replied George "I hope Bung is OK."

"So do I" answered Harry "Not sure that Fart will be much help though."

   Harry decided to park in a lay-by a good hundred yards away from the farm and cautiously walk the rest of the way. The storm had long gone, rolling its way eastwards down the Mediterranean. There was no moon and the cliffs of Dingli were pitch black. The silence of the night was deafening. Nothing stirred.

"We will go in from the back" instructed Harry "I will call Bung on his walkie talkie. If I call his mobile it will light up and give his position away."

"Good thinking" whispered George.

The farm was surrounded by a seven foot high traditionally built Maltese stone wall. It was two feet thick and could withstand anything. Although it was referred to as a farm in actual fact it was just a one room stone building with no windows and an outside staircase leading to a flat roof. Several outbuildings had been used to house a herd of goats and there was a small grain store with a large tank to collect rain water.

Pawlu had worked hard to convert the outbuildings into state of the art 'doggy digs'– as he liked to call them. He had converted the room into an office and built a desk for Bungalow to use as head security guard and had put in a toilet and hand basin. He had also constructed a wire cage within the walls to keep the dogs from straying and to give them freedom to get some exercise.

"Where are you?" Harry called Bungalow on the walkie talkie. Bungalow's walkie talkie crackled into life.

"Hello, Hello. Calling Harry. Calling Harry. Can you hear me?" Bung pressed the transmit button.

"Loud and clear" responded Harry "Are you OK? Where are you? Over."

"I am outside the wall on the cliff edge" answered Bungalow "I heard a noise earlier on. Think someone was trying to break in. Having a look around. Over."

"Roger. Message received. Be careful" replied Harry.

"No, its Bung, I said I am following footsteps. Who is Roger? Over."

"Never mind about Roger. I think I heard them too. Sounds like they are heading for the gate. I have George with me. Over."

"Come on George" Harry whispered "They are heading for the gate. Bungalow is following them. Let's go."

No sooner had they set off than George went sprawling head over heels falling flat on his face.

"You OK, George? What happened?" Harry helped his friend to his feet.

"Tripped on something. I'm OK" said George dusting himself down "It was this pole thing. Who left that there?"

"No, that's a fishing net. I think it belongs to Pawlu. Hey, that could come in handy. Bring it with you."

"Calling Bung. Calling Bung" Harry was on the walkie talkie again "Are you near the gate yet, over?"

"Hi Mr Harry" replied Bungalow "Yes nearly there. Over."

"Roger Bung. So are we."

"No I told you. This is Bungalow. You know, you're security guard. Who is this Roger? I am on my own. Is he with you?" Bungalow was clearly confused.

"Forget Roger. Keep your voice down. George has got Pawlu's fishing net so we can use it to catch the intruder. Roger and Out."

"Mr Harry I think I am getting interference from someone called Roger. Over."

"I said forget Roger. We have the net. I am near the gateway. I can hear someone the other side of the wall. Get ready. We are at the gate now."

"So am I. Over" answered Bungalow.

"Wait for my command Bung" instructed Harry.

"Get ready George. Be careful. I can see a silhouette" Harry whispered to George.

As the figure appeared in the gateway Harry shouted to George to throw the net over him.

"Now, George. Go for it" screamed Harry. He launched himself at the intruder with all his might and between them they fought him to the ground.

"Sit on him" ordered Harry with which command George duly obliged. Harry grabbed the walkie talkie.

"Come in Bung. Where are you? Over."

"Help Harry, He's attacked me. Where are you? He is sitting on me. I can't move. Get George. Get Roger" screamed Bungalow.

"For crying out loud Bung" exclaimed George who suddenly realised that the arch criminal that he was sitting on was none other than Bungalow himself.

"What the heck is going on Bung" said Harry "Where is the burglar? What are you doing in the net?"

"I don't know" answered Bung "One minute I was following the footsteps, next I was pounced on and trapped in Pawlu's fishing net."

George stood up and helped the unfortunate Bungalow to his feet.

"What a load of idiots we are" laughed George."We thought you were the intruder and you thought we were. We've been chasing each other's footsteps! We've all been on a wild goose chase."

"I didn't see a goose" Bungalow was puzzled "Maybe it belongs to Roger."

"There is no goose Bung and no Roger. Just some complete twits – namely you, me and George."

"But what about this Roger person. Has he escaped as well?"

"Bung. Believe me. There was no Roger, there was no goose, there was no intruder. Come on let's get the kettle on and have a coffee to steady our nerves. I need it after all that. By the way where is Fart?"

"I put him in the compound with the dogs to protect them" answered Bungalow.

Harry couldn't believe what he was hearing.

"You did what?" he exclaimed

"It is OK" said Bungalow "Fart likes the greyhounds. They play well together."

"I bet they do" Harry was very angry "Get him out of there before he does any damage."

   Harry was beside himself. All that effort, all that investment, his dream of a pedigree line of racing dogs could have been destroyed by that arch trouble maker, Fart.

"If Fart has had his wicked way with Her Ladyship then... then..." fumed Harry.

"Take it easy Harry" said George trying to calm Harry but not being convinced himself "Nothing may have happened. You know Fart is the laziest creature on this earth."

"I certainly hope so" Harry was less trusting "Not a word of this to anyone George. It is important."

"I know. I know. My lips are sealed."

"I am sorry Mr Harry. But I really did think I heard someone" explained Bungalow, dusting himself down.

Harry was calming down now.

"It's OK Bung old chap. You were only doing your job. Better that we make fools of ourselves than anything bad happens. Let's just sort out Fart."

Harry made straight for the compound only to find Fart fast asleep near the gate. There was no sound from the other dogs.

"See I told you Harry" said George "Nothing to worry about. The dogs are safe."

"I hope so George. I hope so" Harry was only half convinced. Bungalow poured the coffees.

"Nice place you have got here" remarked George "Very plush. Coffee machine, bed for a siesta and your own ensuite. Home from home. Pawlu has done a good job."

"Thank you" said Bungalow "I have my own desk as well."

Bungalow was clearly very pleased with his new found importance. Indeed Pawlu had worked wonders with what had been a derelict building.

"Well, what a night! In fact what a day" said Harry "First I nearly get struck with lightning and then all these shenanigans. What next I wonder."

"All part of life's rich pattern" laughed George "Anyway look on the bright side. No-one got hurt and the dogs are OK. All's well that ends well. Right?"

"Unlike you to be so positive George but you are right" mused Harry "Although I still have my doubts about the nocturnal activities of Fart. Look at him. He has a self satisfied grin on his face if ever I saw one. If he has had his wicked way with her Ladyship, then, well, then I don't know what we are going to do."

"No good crying about it until we know for sure" advised George "Put it to the back of your mind and let nature take its course."

"That's all very well but it is the course of nature that worries me. Anyway, I know what we have to do now. We must get some security cameras so you can monitor what is going on from your desk Bung and I must get your driving lessons organised as soon as possible."

Nothing else to do now but for Harry and George go home and leave Bungalow and Fart to do their duty – although Harry feared that maybe, just maybe Fart had gone beyond the call of duty.

Harry was a bag of nerves as the consequences of Fart's exploits began to sink in. The pedigrees of Lord Nodagan and Her Ladyship may have been compromised. If that was the case then goodness knows what the pups would like like! Who ever heard of a hairy greyhound?

Would they have big, fat pot bellies? What would the Mayor say when he found out? What would Joan think? He would not be able to look his neighbours in the eye. Harry was in for a sleepless night.

Neither Harry nor George spoke on the road back to Ħal-Luqa.

# What's up with Thursday!

Just as the church bells of St Andrew's rang out to warn the villagers of Ħal-Luqa that it was six thirty, so, true to form the three pals entered the Ho Chi Do Chi bar as they had done for the last ten years.

"Hi Ho" said Harry, first over the door step.

"Hi Ho" said George.

"Hi Ho" said Aris.

"Good evening my flends" replied Ho as he poured their drinks. Like all good bar men he knew the favourite drink of each of his regular drinkers.

The ritual of greeting having been completed the trio sat in their respective chairs, sized up their glasses of their preferred beer – Blue Label for Harry, Hop Leaf for George and Cisk for Aris and in unison they slowly downed the thirst quenching nectar that they enjoyed so much and which gave Ho and the brewery a good living .

Ho Chi who had travelled from Hong Kong with his wife Do and their children Din and Don, nearly ten years ago had settled into village life and was well accepted by the villagers. Neither Ho nor Do had mastered the Maltese language even though Do had made a valiant attempt to do so. The fact that she had tried had warmed her to the hearts of the Maltese.

Indeed they had contributed greatly to the social activities of the village when they took over the bar from old Joe. Joe was in his eighties and although he went through the routine of opening and closing the bar on time, his heart was not in it. The Chi's were a breath of fresh air and with Ho's innovations and Do's diligence the bar soon became a thriving business and was the place to go in  Ħal–Luqa.

"So, what's up with you Harry" asked George "You've got a face on that would turn the milk sour."

"Nothing really" groaned Harry.

"Sorry, not buying it. Something's up" said George "Come on spit it out."

"No honestly, nothing. Just a bit bored I guess, after all it is Thursday" answered Harry.

"What has Thursday got to do with it?" asked Aris.

"Well its Thursday, isn't it?" replied Harry.

"And!" said Aris, still waiting for an explanation.

"Well, Thursday is a nothing day isn't it?" said Harry "Not like a Tuesday or Wednesday."

"You've lost me" said George "When you're retired, every day is the same as far as I am concerned."

"Well, no. Not really" Harry replied "Monday is a lost day because it is the day for recovering from the weekend. But Tuesday and Wednesday are the days when you can get things done. New plans. New schemes. New ideas. But Thursday is a nothing day because you've done all the work on Tuesday and Wednesday and tomorrow is Friday when nobody does anything because the weekend is coming up."

"I see your point" said George sarcastically "What you are describing is 'apathy'. Plain and simple. If you're saying that the whole World is reduced to a two day week then we are all in trouble."

"Personally I see nothing wrong with a bit of apathy" said Aris. "The world is going too fast. If people were a bit more laid back then there would be less stress, less depression and less people going off the rails."

"I'll drink to that" said George raising his pint.

"Everyone is chasing a target nowadays' continued Aris "If you made five grand last year you are expected to make six grand this year. Why? If you can get a good living out of five then why break a gut trying for more. It is just plain greed in my book."

"You are beginning to sound like George" said Harry.

"He's right though Harry" joined in George "That's why we are all stressed. Look at you for example. I've never known you so depressed."

"Take no notice of me" smiled Harry "I guess all this greyhound stuff and the stadium are getting to me."

"Oh! Come on Harry. You should be happy as a sand boy" said Aris trying to cheer him up.

 "The kennels are done. Pawlu has done a great job. You have two fine specimens of greyhounds. The bitch with a bit of luck will produce her first litter. Everything is going exactly to plan. What is worrying you? The other day you were full of it. Now you are back in your miserable mode."

"Yes, you are right. I am right old misery, aren't I?" said Harry realising that he must put on a brave face lest he gave his big secret away. The image of a grinning Fart as he had his way with Her Ladyship kept appearing before him. Harry shook his head to shake off the thought. "Set up another round Ho. Let's get the place cheered up."

"Ah! Here's Bungalow and Fart. Just in time. What are you having Bung old chap?"

"Thank you Mr Harry" said Bungalow "But I am on duty at the kennels this evening. I better not drink."

  Bungalow who had taken to his duty as kennel guard very seriously was resplendent in his guard's uniform which Harry had provided. He wore his camouflage trousers, black T shirt and red beret with great pride. Fart was equally impressed with is new appointment as guard dog.

"I just came in to tell you I was on my way" said Bungalow "My
bus will be coming soon."

As Bungalow prepared to catch his bus Aris remarked that it
would probably take him over an hour to get to Dingli by bus and
then he would have a quarter of a mile walk.

"You are right. It is quite a journey for him" said Harry "He has
never complained. Anyway I am doing something about it. I am
going to fix him up with some wheels."

"Does he have a driving licence?" asked Aris.

"No, but I have applied for a provisional licence for him" replied
Harry "He has some experience of driving albeit illegal. I know he
drives on his dad's farm."

"Good on you Harry" said Aris "You can pick up an old banger for
him for peanuts. He will be made up. Has he never applied for a
licence?"

"Not that I know of" said Harry "Better make sure."

Harry called out to Bungalow as he left the bar.

"Hold on a minute Bung old chap" called Harry "Have you ever
had a driving licence?"

"I don't think so" answered Bungalow.

"Mmm. My guess is that you haven't. I will apply for a provisional
one and get some driving lessons organised" said Harry "Leave it
to me."

"Thank you Mr Harry" Bungalow was very pleased. He really was
going up in the world.

"Good man" said Harry "Have a peaceful night."

As Bungalow set off to do his duty so Aris turned to Harry.

"I tell you what Harry" he said "If you are OK with it, I will give Bungalow some driving lessons. We can use my old Morris."
"Are you sure Aris? That is most generous of you" said Harry "It might be a tougher job than you think."
"He'll be OK with me. Don't worry" Aris smiled.
"See Harry" said George "Thursday is not so boring after all. You have been presented with a problem and have resolved to solve it. A useful and productive day after all, don't you think?"
"You're right George. As usual" Harry smiled "Another round over here Ho. Let's drink a few beers to Thursday."
After all tomorrow is Friday!

# Shocking News

"Why do I feel so cold" complained Angus "I thought people came to Malta in January to escape the cold of England."
"Ah! You are turning into an old softy in your old age" laughed Joan.

   But Angus was right. Malta can feel very cold in the early months of winter even though the temperature reads around eight or nine degrees. It is not so much the temperature that makes people feel cold as the dampness. Malta is a large piece of limestone rock just about sticking up out of the Mediterranean sea. It is surrounded by water thus mak ng the air humid. The limestone does not retain any heat and absorbs the dampness like a great sponge. It is this dampness that soaks into the very bones that makes them feel so cold.

"I've lived through more than sixty Scottish winters but I have never felt this cold" continued Angus.

"Your memory is playing tricks on you Angus. It is a different sort of cold that's all" countered Joan "In Scotland you would have your thermal vest, a shirt, a couple of pullovers, jacket and top coat. Here you still think it is summer. One shirt and a pullover! It is psychological. You expect Malta to be hot all the time so you are not prepared for it when it is not."

"So you are saying I am crazy now, are you!" chuckled Angus.

"Aye, well, I won't answer that" laughed Joan.

Angus and Joan had decided to sell up in Scotland and move to Malta when Angus retired and when Joan had her windfall from Aunty Alice. It was a good decision as Angus had heart problems and suffered from arthritis. The Maltese climate helped both conditions even though early winter was so damp. They had bought a small house in Tarxien Road which was close to the centre of the village.

Harry was delighted that his 'sis' as he now chose to call her, had made the decision to relocate to Malta. He had lost touch with her for many years and this was his chance to catch up with her and her family. The pair had settled in to Maltese life like ducks to water and the villagers had welcomed them. In fact they loved to hear Angus's Scottish accent. The way he rolled his r's and spoke with such clarity. But then he was from Aberdeen where everyone speaks with perfect diction. Angus always said that it was the folk of Aberdeen who put the 'art' into 'articulation'. And he was right. His careful use of words was greatly appreciated by the Maltese who themselves, never wasted a letter in their language.

Although Angus had retired since coming to Ħal-Luqa he had been very busy working with Joan and Harry on their grand project– the kennels and the greyhound stadium. Angus had volunteered to help with the care and training of the dogs once they were born.  He was reading everything he could get his hands on about greyhounds. Together with Idaho Joe they had a worked out a plan and a schedule for the dog's future. Harry was most impressed and had left them to it since he had no idea what to do. In fact he was beginning to think he had bitten off more than he could chew! But with reassurances from Angus and Idaho and the sisterly support of Joan, he did his best to put on a positive face. The less said the better.

It was the last Friday of the month which meant that young Tonio Marozzi would be performing at the Ho Chi Do Chi Bar with his jazz band – the Tony Marozzi All Star Jazz band. It was not long after Ho and Do had bought the bar that Tonio asked Ho if he could practice in Ho's back room. He had no hesitation and before long the band was performing every Friday night in the bar. So successful were they that fans came from all parts of the island to listen. The band played traditional jazz which is a rarity on the island and their lead singer was Sandra Scicluna. Tonio and Sandra had since married to the delight of everyone especially their parents who had always considered the union as inevitable. The bar was filling up as Angus and Joan arrived.

"Hi Angus. Over here" called Harry "What are you having? G&T for you, sis?"

"Aye. A large Scotch please Harry" answered Angus rubbing his hands together "I need something to warrm me up, d'ye ken."

"Hello Tonio" greeted Joan "Is Sandra going to sing for us tonight?"

"I think so" said Tonio "She may come in later but she was not feeling too well. A touch of the winter blues I guess."

"Well if anyone knows about the blues it is your Sandra" remarked Aris. "She is one of the best blues singer I have ever heard. I love her version of Beale Street Blues. Will she sing it tonight?"

"I'm sure she will if you ask her Aris" replied Tonio.

"So, it won't be long now then, Tonio" remarked George.

"Yes, you're right I must drink up" answered Tonio "The rest of the band will be here soon. Better get set up."

George laughed. Joan smiled and nodded a wink at Harry.

"Never mind the band" he said "You have more important matters to think about."

"I have?" Tonio was puzzled.

"Of course you have. I said forget the band, what about your lovely wife and the pending arrival of your son and heir."

"Ah yes! I forgot" said Tonio embarrassed that he had not realised what George was getting at.

"Forgot!" exclaimed George "Probably the biggest thing that will happen in your life and you forgot!"

"Take no notice Tonio" said Joan "You're not the first one to forget. In any case for a man a baby is not really real until it is born. Isn't that right Carmena?"

"*Veru*" said Carmena "For the mother the unborn baby is real from the first moment she feels him move. But for the man he is nothing until the moment of birth."

As the ladies in the bar huddled together to discuss 'babies', a subject close to all their hearts and one which no man would dare to interfere with or offer an opinion on, the men ordered more drinks and sat back waiting for the music to start.

The band had kept the same line up since it had started with the exception of Paul Baker the lead trumpet. Paul had finished his tour of duty at the airport and had returned to the UK. It left the band without a lead. Tonio was distraught as without a trumpet up front the band would have to fold. It was then that Johnny Azzopardi, the bands energetic drummer introduced a lad from Birkakara who played a saxophone. He was a member of the very well respected St Helena band.

Tonio was unsure about a lead sax but after a few sessions he changed his mind. His name was Leli Schembri and was a distant relative of Johnny. His love of trad jazz made him an ideal addition. The future of the band was secured.

The bar was by now full of regulars and faithful followers of the Tony Marozzi All Star Jazz band. They kicked off the session with their signature tune 'Tiger Rag' followed by Muskrat Ramble and St Louis Blues. It was going to be a great night.

"Have you warmed up yet Angus?" asked Harry.

"Aye, I have" answered Angus raising his glass "Thanks to the whisky and the wonderrful company."

"Are you hinting that you want a refill" asked Harry laughing.

"I wouldny say no" replied Angus

"He never says No" added Joan.

"Purely medicinal, my love. Purely medicinal. Good for the heart don't ye know." chuckled Angus tapping his chest.

Just then Sandra entered with her dad, Mario and her in-laws Carmen and Salvu, the parents of Tonio.

"Over here" called Pawlu "Come and sit with your Aunty Carmena." Carmena clutching her black plastic handbag shuffled up to make room for them.

"How are you Sandra?" she asked "I see you are getting close. When is it due?"

"Not until the second week of February" said a blushing Sandra.

"I bet you can't wait, can you Carmen?" said Pawlu.

"It will be our first grandchild" answered Carmen "Of course I can't wait."

"Are you going to sing tonight Sandra?" asked George.

"If you want" she replied "It might be my last one for a while. I will be too busy once this one arrives" replied Sandra tapping her tummy.

Sandra made her way up to the stage where the band had just finished a stirring rendition of Basin Street Blues.

"Ladies and Gentlemen" announced Tonio "Please welcome to the stage, my wife, the lovely Sandra accompanied by our soon to be son or daughter."

A great cheer rang out as Sandra took the mic.

"Thank you everyone. Thank you" she blushed "I hope the band don't tell me off but I would like to sing a number that is not trad jazz."

A great crescendo of off tune blasts came from the band as they signalled their disapproval.

"Sacrilege" cried Aris thumping his purple Bass.

"It is '*When you wish upon a Star*', I hope you like it."

The bar was silent mesmerised by the gentle tone of Sandra's angelic voice. The villagers of Ħal-Luqa loved to hear her sing. She had the soul of Billie Holiday, the precision of Ottilie Patterson and the power of Ella Fitzgerald.

"I reckon we should propose Sandra as Malta's next Eurovision contestant. I am sure she could win it" said George.

"I am with you there George" said Harry. "By the way has anyone seen Idaho? He should have been here by now."

"The last I saw of him was getting into Lorretta's taxi" said Pawlu

"He said he had to check something at the kennels."

"Wonder what that is all about" Harry was puzzled.

Sandra finished her song to thunderous applause.

"Encore. Encore. One more Sandra" they called.

"OK" she said "Last one. But this time a real Trad number."

She clicked her fingers and Tonio knew exactly what to play. Johnny Azzopardi launched into a frantic drum solo which had everyone on their feet. At the signal from Tonio the band struck up with '*Mamma don't allow*'. The bar went wild.

Constable Alfred could hear them from the far side of the pjazza and even old Guisseppa in Triq San Gużepp raised an eyebrow as she closed the shutters to fend of what she considered to be the devil's music. Even Harry was up on his feet, jigging away happy in the knowledge that he would not be overwhelmed by the attentions of the ample Marella.

No-one heard Lorretta's taxi pull up outside the bar. Idaho Joe and Lorretta spotted Harry dancing or rather prancing across the floor with Carmena still clutching her black plastic handbag. As the music stopped to the roar of applause from the patrons, Idaho made a direct line for Harry.

"Hey Joe. Where have you been? You are missing a great night" said Harry.

"I know. I know, I can see that" said Joe "But it is going to get even greater, mate. I have some wonderful news Harry."

The bar fell silent.

"Go on. What's happened?" asked Harry.

"I've just come from the kennels and the vet tells me that Her Ladyship is with pups."

Harry was dumbfounded. He sat down with a bump at the news. This is what he had been waiting for.

"Are you sure?" asked George.

"Sure I'm sure" said Idaho with a great grin.

"That is fantastic news Harry" said Joan giving her brother a big hug.

"You're telling me" Harry could hardly believe it "The dream is really coming true Joan. Lord Nodagan has done his duty."

"Dlinks on the house" announced Ho as he started pouring drinks as fast as he and Do could manage.

The bar was alight with happiness and anticipation. Everyone was so happy with Harry's wonderful news.

"When will they be born?" asked Carmena.

"Well the gestation period is usually about sixty three days so the vet reckons it will be on the 10th February" replied Joe.

"Tenth of February! But that is when me and Sandra expect our baby" said Tonio "What a coincidence."

The bar erupted into another crescendo of applause and laughter.

"A double celebration to look forward to" said Mario.

   Out of the corner of his eye Harry noticed that Fart, Bungalow's trusty mongrel had left his kennel the *Villa Tal Kelb Tas-Siġġiewi* and was standing in the doorway of the bar. Harry's blood ran cold. Terror struck his heart. Sixty three days the vet said, Harry began counting. The lightning had struck the *Kappella Tal-Irdum* on the tenth of December. So that means twenty two days in December, plus thirty one days in January. That is fifty three. Fifty three less sixty three is....... "Oh No".

"What's up Harry? You've gone white as a sheet" said George.

Harry pulled George aside.

"I have just worked it out. The birth will be sixty three days since we went to find that intruder at Dingli" explained Harry.

"So" said George.

"So! So! Don't you remember that was when Bungalow left Fart alone with Her Ladyship. The tenth of December. It is too much of a coincidence" cried Harry reaching for his drink.

"Ok, Keep calm. Don't say anything" advised George "We know nothing yet. Wait 'til they are born. Then, well, then we panic!"

"You're a great help" said Harry "How am I going to get through the next few weeks not knowing. I was already feeling depressed now I'm positively suicidal. Besides you know when the tenth of February is don't you?"

"No. Not particularly" queried George.

"It is the day of St Paul's shipwreck at Selmunet. A disaster. Just like this one" Harry was distraught. There was no consoling him.

"Listen" said George firmly "Pull yourself together man. Put on a brave face and let fate take its course."

"Haven't got much choice have I?" lamented Harry.

The evening over, the bar was emptying. Everyone was congratulating Harry who was doing his very best to put on a happy face. As Harry and George were the last to leave George put a comforting arm around his old pals shoulder.

"Don't worry Harry, it will be all right" he said.

   Fart was still at the doorway and George could not help but notice that the animal seemed to have a grin that stretched from one jowl to the other.

What did he know? That dog had an uncanny way of knowing what was going on. George felt a cold shiver run through his body!

The bells summoning the good citizens of Ħal-Luqa to early morning Mass, the rooster waking up those who preferred to spend a few more minutes in bed, the blaring horn of the bread van as he announced his arrival, all signalled the start of another day.

Lucia, Harry's loyal housekeeper had already been to church and was preparing breakfast for Harry as he stumbled into the kitchen.

"What's up with you, Harry? You look like death warmed up" she remarked.

"I'm alright Lucia. Didnt sleep too well that's all" groaned Harry.

"Unlike you" she replied "You can usually sleep on a clothes line. What's up?"

"Everytime I went to close my eyes this image of Fart's ugly face appeared, grinning from ear to ear" complained Harry.

"Fart! Our lovely Fart! He wouldn't hurt a fly. What's that all about?" asked Lucia.

"It's nothing. Just me" Harry dodged the question " A couple of pieces of toast and a coffee and I will be fine."

Lucia had already put the thick slices of Maltese bread under the grill. She deliberately let the bread burn as Harry liked his toast well and truly cremated. She spread an extra thick layer of butter and marmalade. Harry was clearly upset about something and a good dose of sugar might help.

"I will take an early siesta today. Anyway it might be wise to keep off the roads today" added Harry.

"Why? What's happening?

"Aris is giving Bung his first driving lesson. Could be risky" advised Harry.

"I will make sure I don't venture out then " said Lucia wisely.

And as it happens, it was just as well she didn't!

# Bung goes for a drive.

"You will continue to drive in a straight line, maintaining this position in the road until I give you your next instruction." Aris was well into his RAF instructor's role as he took Bungalow on his first driving lesson.

It was Harry who had suggested that Bungalow should get a driving licence for although Bung had driven his father's tractors since he was a boy, he had never taken his test on the road. If Bungalow was to be the security guard at the Dingli kennels then it followed that a driving licence would be an asset.

Bungalow was keen to learn and Aris had no hesitation in offering his services as driving instructor. He was even prepared to make available his treasured Morris Oxford estate for the lessons.

"Are you sure you know what you are letting yourself in for?" asked George.

"It will be OK. I will keep him in check" said Aris "Why? What do you know that I don't?"

"Nothing really" said George "Except that his Dad told me that when he was twelve he left the brake off one tractor and it plunged into the quarry at Għar Lapsi and then when he was fifteen he lost control of another tractor which ended up careering over the cliffs at Wied Iż-Żurrieq and is now at the bottom of the Med! Other than that I know nothing."

"Well, he is older and wiser now. I will take my chances" replied Aris, albeit with some trepidation.

So it was that Aris had taken Bungalow to the airfield perimeter road at Safi. The afternoon was hot but calm and peaceful. Aris had deliberately chosen to take the drive mid afternoon when most people would be enjoying their siestas. The roads were empty of traffic and this seemed an ideal time to judge the competence of his charge. So far so good. Bung had mastered the controls and was driving at a comfortable speed. Fart, Bungalow's faithful dog, had settled himself on the back seat and was enjoying the ride – as far as a dog knows what a ride is!

"At the next junction you will take a left turn" said Aris in his most authoritive voice. He had not been a Flight Sargeant for nothing!

To Aris's utter dismay, Bungalow immediately swung the steering wheel hard over to the left, at the same time pressing the accelerator pedal hard to the floor. With an ear splitting screech of the tyres the car swung off the road and through the open doors of the entrance to the Lidl supermarket. Fart dived for cover in the footwell between the seats. Swerving and speeding over the marble floor the car demolished the entire vegetable section spewing fruit and vegetables everywhere. Potatoes, carrots, cauliflowers, turnips flying through the air.  Customers ran for their lives. In terrified panic ladies picked up their skirts, scooped up their children, clutched their bags and ran for the exits.

Bungalow was transfixed. His hands frozen to the steering wheel. His eyes staring ahead but seeing nothing. Aris could not believe what was happening.
"When I said turn left, I meant at the next junction– not Lidl's front doors" he screamed.

Bungalow did not hear him. He was in another world completely mesmerised by the scene unfolding around him. His foot firmly pressed on the accelerator the car continued to crash into the food counters spewing breakfast cereal, biscuits, tins of peas, fruit and spices around the aisles.

Aris realised he had to do something. Grabbing the hand brake with both hands he wrenched it hard on. The car immediately went into a spin, taking out the dairy counter, the delicatessen and the drinks counters in one fell swoop. Cartons of milk, yoghurt, custard burst open spraying their contents across the supermarket floor, soaking any unfortunate customers in the way and completely covering Aris's pride and joy. His beautifully cared for green and wood-grain estate car was now an unrecognisable mixture of jellies, blancmange, whipped cream and yoghurt. Cartons of raspberry, blackcurrant and orange juice spurted their contents into the melee creating a wonderful cocktail of  whipped cream, blancmange and custard making  the biggest knickerbocker glory ever seen.

By now the car had come to rest. Fortunately for Aris, it was pointing towards the main doors. Aris grabbed Bungalow by the shoulders, heaved him out of the driving seat and took over the controls. Bungalow raced round to the passenger side slipping and sliding in the rivers of milk and yoghurt. Aris selected second gear and gently let out the clutch until the spinning wheels eventually took grip in the flooded marble floor. Gathering speed he sped directly to the exit, spun back into the road and headed for home leaving behind a scene of utter chaos and destruction.

It was still mid afternoon and the road was clear. The villagers of Kirkop and Luqa were still rising from their afternoon sleep. Aris was keen to get under cover as quickly as possible before anyone saw him. He need not have worried as the car was now covered in cream, custard, yoghurt and fruit and vegetables. It was unrecognisable as a car! Indeed as Aris sped along the perimeter road the 4p.m. flight from London Gatwick was landing.  The passengers looked in total disbelief at what appeared to be a massive pink and orange meringue with a pineapple on top speeding along parallel to the runway. For the first time visitor to the island it was sight of great amusement and amazement. To the seasoned traveller it was– well, it was Malta.

Aris was debating what his next course of action should be. As far as he was aware no one had identified his car. He had not seen anyone in the streets. So far so good. First priority must be to remove all trace of the mishmash of creams, jellies, yoghurts and fruit that covered the car.

As he pulled into Luqa village he noticed that Di Marco's self service car wash was open. Quick as a flash he swerved into the garage. Thankfully the place was deserted.

"Bungalow" he shouted "Start washing every trace of Lidl from the car. We have to remove anything that may incriminate us.Hurry. No time to lose."

Fortunately the mixture that covered the car easily washed off and dissolved as it ran down the drains.

"Hose under the wheel arches and underneath the car" he ordered Bungalow.

Once every trace of the event had been removed, Aris ordered Bung back into the car and he drove to his garage which he had fortunately left open. Screeching to a stop, he turned off the engine and slumped back into his seat.

"Shut the doors" he commanded Bungalow.

"Phew! That was something I would not want to do everyday" said Aris.

"I am sorry Mr Aris but I misunderstood you. Next time I will do it properly" said Bungalow.

"Next Time! Next time! What makes you think there will be a next time" screamed Aris. "Sorry Bung old chap. But that is it. You book in with a driving school next time. I can't go through that again."

"OK. I understand. What shall we do next?" he asked.

"Well one thing we don't do is admit that we were driving anywhere near Safi this afternoon" said Aris.

"OK.  Where shall we say we were driving?" asked Bungalow.

"No. No. We say nothing. As far as anyone is concerned we have not been out in the car at all. Understand?"

"OK. OK.  I say nothing to no-one."

"Good. Now I reckon we should go to Ho's bar and get a drink. I know I need it" said Aris.

"Ah! No need." Bungalow went to the back of the car "Look I have a dozen bottles of La Valette here. We can open one. Huh!" said Bungalow clearly pleased with himself.

Aris looked in disbelief.

"Where did they come from? And what is all that other stuff?" Aris was dismayed as he saw not only the crate of wine but a couple of shoulders of lamb, several tins of beans and peas, sausages- enough to keep Fart happy for months and a cauliflower.

"When we swopped seats I noticed that the customers who were running for cover were filling their shopping bags with what they could grab, so I thought I would join them" explained Bungalow as if it was quite acceptable to do so.

"But that is stealing, Bungalow" Aris was now very angry and dismayed as he realised the enormity of what they had done.

"No. No. No. We must keep calm. Let's think this through. We have to be very careful or we will end up in jail."

Aris was contemplating the options as he spoke.

"We could return the goods. But that would mean admitting what we had done. No good. We can deny everything and split the bounty and have that on our consciences for the rest of our lives" reasoned Aris.

"What if...." began Bungalow.

"Shush. Let me think" said Aris raising his hand to silence Bungalow while he thought about it. "As far as we know, no one saw us. Once the car was covered in cream it was unidentifiable. With all the products that were stolen, no one is going to know what we took and anyway we can say we bought if from somewhere else."

"And if we keep quiet no one will know" added Bungalow.

"Well. That's it. We keep quiet and deny everything. Look amazed when the gossip starts, and go about our business as if nothing happened" Aris had decided that this was the best course of action.

"Bungalow, I think we deserve that drink now" at last Aris smiled "You know what Bung old chap, that was the most excitement I have had in years."

Aris clasped Bungalow's hand and shook it warmly as they both broke out into uncontrollable laughter. There was nothing more to do now than to repair to Ho's bar for that drink.

"Good afternoon Ho" greeted Aris entering the bar.

"Good Afternoon Mr Alis" replied Ho "You are in good spilits today I think. Are you cereblating something? Is it your birthday?"

"No" replied Aris "Nothing like that my friend. Just two good friends in need of a drink. Set them up please. A Cisk for me and whatever Bungalow wants."

As Ho poured the drinks they were joined by Harry and George.

"Get the usual for these two Ho" said Aris.

"Thanks Aris" said Harry "Very kind of you. You are a bit early today Aris. What have you been up to?" he asked.

"Up to! Up to! Er nothing, nothing at all" said Aris defensively.

"Mmm. Do I smell a whiff of mendacity Harry? I think Aris is hiding something" said George.

"What me? Never. Straight as a die. Always have been. No. No. It has been a quiet day for me. Nothing to speak of" replied Aris defensively.

"And it has been a quiet day for me too" added Bungalow.

"So you were helping each other have a quiet day were you?" asked George.

"I just happened to bump into Bungalow this afternoon and we took Fart for a walk. Nice and peaceful. Nothing unusual happened" explained Aris.

"Nothing unusual at all" Bungalow confirmed Aris's rather weak explanation.

"So you helped each other to do nothing unusual. Is that right?" asked George.

"Of course. Nothing unusual happened. What is unusual about that? What is this? The inquisition!" Aris was getting agitated

"Nothing unusual happened. That is it. Now please can we have our drink in peace and change the subject."

"Calm down Aris. Calm down. If nothing unusual happened then nothing unusual happened. No need to get up tight about nothing unusual happening. It happens all the time".

"What does?" asked Bungalow.

"Nothing unusual of course "said George with a mischievous grin. He knew there was more to this than Ar s or Bungalow were letting on.

"Leave it George" Harry intervened as he saw Aris getting hot under the collar. "If nothing unusual happened then that is what happened. Let's talk about something e se."

"OK. Sorry Aris. You know what I am like when it comes to winding people up. I apologise" said George.

As they turned to their drinks a very excited Pawlu came rushing into the bar.

"Hi guys" he said "have you seen the news on TV?"

"News. What news?" asked Harry.

"This afternoon. Something unusual happened at the Lidl supermarket."

"Really" said George his ears pricking up. "I wonder if that was the same something unusual that happened to you Aris."

"Where you there Aris?" asked Palwu.

"No we were not anywhere near Safi this afternoon" said Bungalow.

"Ah! " said George "The  plot thickens. Who said anything about Safi ? "

Bungalow looked at Aris. Aris frowned but kept his head down.

"So what happened then?" asked Harry.

"It seems some madmen drove a truck into Lidl's Safi supermarket and got away with thousands of pounds worth of goods and caused mass destruction of the counters and showcases."

"Was anyone hurt?" asked Harry.

"No. Thank goodness. But an eye witness said that there were two of them and they looked like very dangerous criminals."

"Can they describe the vehicle?" asked George.

"No. I don't think so. It all happened so quickly" explained Pawlu.

"Well now. That really is a very unusual thing to happen, isn't it Aris?" said George.

Aris declined to answer.

"What do you make of it Bungalow?" teased George.

"I do not know what happened as I was not there. So I cannot comment" replied Bungalow "I was doing nothing unusual with Mr Aris at the time."

"What time would that be then" asked George.

"About two thirty" replied Bungalow.

Aris winced.

"Bonjornu, gentlemen" Constable Alfred Ellul appeared in the doorway of the bar.

"Ah! Constable Alfred" said Ho. "What can I get you to dlink?"

"Nothing for me thank you Ho. Not when I am on duty" replied the constable. "I would just like a quick chat with my friends over here."

The constable pulled up a chair close to where Bungalow was sitting.

"Gentlemen" he said looking directly at Aris. "How are we all this afternoon? Nothing unusual happening I hope."

The constable reached into his bag and placed a pineapple on the table.

"Nothing unusual at all, constable" replied George on behalf of them all "Why do you ask?"

"Have you not seen the news?" asked the constable.

"News? What news" asked Harry beginning to cotton on to what George had already worked out.

" It appears that around two thirty this afternoon  a couple of reprobates smashed their way into Lidl's supermarket at Safi and caused thousands of pounds worth of damage before racing off towards Ħal-Luqa" explained the constable.

"Why would anyone do that?" asked Harry clearly puzzled as to what the motive could have been.

"Anyone's guess I suppose" said the constable "But a lot of produce was stolen during the chaos. It may have been a put up job."

"Where there any witnesses" asked Harry.

"It seems that the vehicle that was used was an old car. It is described as being green in colour with doors at the back made of wood"

"Sounds a bit like your car Aris" laughed Pawlu.

"No. No. Not possible. My car has not left the garage for a week. Battery flat, you see" replied Aris thinking quickly.

"So I can safely say that you were nowhere near the Lidl supermarket this afternoon. Is that right Aris?" enquired the constable.

"What! Aris in a supermarket" exclaimed George "He lives on cornflakes, pork pies and Cisk! Why would he go to a supermarket? I doubt if he has ever been to a supermarket in his entire life! Don't make me laugh."

Aris was grateful for the interruption.

"And what about you Bungalow? Were you in Safi this afternoon?"

"No sir" replied Bungalow "I was doing nothing unusual in Siġġiewi."

"Can anyone verify that for you?"  the constable probed.

"Yes. Mr Aris was helping me" answered Bungalow .

"Helping you! Helping you to do what?"

"Nothing unusual sir" Bungalow was getting nervous. He looked at Aris for support.

"So, you were both very busy doing nothing unusual. It must have taken you all afternoon then."

"What are you getting at constable?" asked Harry "Aris and Bung are fine upstanding members of the community. Why are you asking these questions? You know that there will be plenty of witnesses to say that they were nowhere near Safi this afternoon if it comes to the crunch."

"About that I have no doubt" sighed the constable.

   Constable Alfred knew he was not going to win. He knew that the entire village would turn up to verify that the suspects were anywhere but in Safi that afternoon, even No Lights. In any case, having been the village constable for nearly ten years now and with the prospect of his retirement in a couple of months, why rock the boat. He loved living in Luqa and intended to make it his retirement home. He would have to get on with his neighbours and feel comfortable having a drink in Ho's bar. If he arrested Aris and Bungalow all that would be finished. After all, no-one was hurt. The supermarket was due for refurbishment anyway and the missing food was no doubt covered by insurance. An immoral attitude perhaps but a practical one. All in all, best to let sleeping dogs lie.

"Well gentlemen. I thank you for your cooperation. If any of you think of anything that might help my enquiries then you know where I am. I bid you good day."

"Oh. I nearly forgot. This pineapple was found outside the doors of your garage Aris. I suppose you have not mislaid one recently have you?"

"No constable. I don't like pineapples. Never eat them in fact" answered Aris.

"Well, I will take your word for it my friend" smiled the constable " Maybe I should hold on to it though as it may prove to be a vital piece of evidence."

"Of course" responded Aris " And if I come across someone looking for a pineapple I will get in touch immediately."

"Yes, I am sure you will" the constable knew it was never going to happen.

The constable raised himself wearily from his chair but in doing so trod heavily on the tail of Fart the dog who had rested himself under the table at feet of his master.

An ear splitting yelp pierced the ears of all in the bar as Fart leapt up, knocking the table over and scattering the beers across the floor. Fart darted for the door clutching what appeared to be string of sausages in his mouth. As he ran a piece of paper fell to the floor.

George, quick thinking as ever, realised it was a Lidl shop label. It had been wrapped around the packet of sausages that Bungalow had liberated from the store. George swiftly covered it with his size eleven shoes before the constable noticed. Smiling at the constable he politely gestured him towards the door. Once the coast was clear he bent down and retrieved the label from the sole of his shoe.

"Now I wonder what this is? Looks like I may have trodden on a vital piece of evidence" he remarked.

"It is a Lidl price tag" said Pawlu "How did that get there?"

"How indeed" said George loving every minute of Aris's discomfort.

"That's enough George. I think we all know that Aris and Bungalow are somehow involved" intervened Harry "If you want to tell us about it Aris, it is up to you otherwise let's get another round in and we will say no more."

"You're a good friend Harry. Thank you" said Aris "Truth is I was giving Bung a driving lesson and he mistakenly thought the entrance to Lidl was a junction and we ended up in rather a mess."

"I'll say you did" laughed George.

"Well we made our escape and if you don't mind I would rather forget about the whole incident" pleaded Aris.

"That is all very well "said George "But a crime has been committed and there is important evidence that indicates exactly who the perpetrators are."

"Evidence? What evidence?" asked Aris.

"This Lidl price tag that I have in my hands. That's what evidence" said George waving the incriminating label in front of Bungalow's face.

"But that proves nothing" said Harry. "He could have bought those sausages at any time and in any case the label was on the floor and could have been dropped by anyone."

"Except that I witnessed it falling from the sausages in Fart's mouth" replied George.

"OK, so Fart is the arch criminal. We should mount a search party for Fart immediately" said Harry.

"And send out search warrants and APB's to all police patrols to look out for  a sinister, black haired mongrel with a string of sausages in his mouth" said Pawlu.

"Do not approach this dog. He may be dangerous" added Harry laughing.

"It is OK Aris. I won't say a word but you must admit it is very amusing. You can tell us the full story later when you have calmed down" said George

"I will. I will" said Aris with a sigh of great relief. "But, I have to say Bungalow that I here and now resign as your driving instructor. I don't think my nerves could not stand another day like that".

"But I thought you said nothing unusual happened" teased George.

"If that was nothing unusual then I dread to think what the usual is" said Aris.

"That is easy" said Ho "The usual is a pint of Cisk" handing a very welcome pint to his friend.

"I'll drink to that Ho. I'll drink to that" said a very relieved Aris.

" Hey Aris' called George from the bar "would you like a piece of pineapple with your drink?

Everyone on the bar started to laugh at George's wind up. Aris nearly choked on his beer.

"If I never see another pineapple in my life it will be too soon" replied Aris.

"So Ho. I think we need to declare the Ho Chi Do Chi Bar a pineapple free zone. What do you say?"said George.

"Ah so!" replied Ho "No pineappoo in bar. I now declare this bar is a pineappoo flee zone."

"And so say all of us" shouted the patrons of teh bar.

A great cheer rang our as Ho rang the bar bell three times.

# Din and Don Come Home

"All he did was to strike a match to light his cigarette, when this whale fell on his head" said Bungalow.

George choked on his beer.

"What are you talking about?" spluttered George.

"It fell on his head. Splattered him all over the pavement."

"Bungalow, just in case you hadn't noticed, whales do not fall on people's heads. Whales do not fly. Whales do not climb ladders and fall off. Whales do not leap from multi storey car parks onto people" explained George "Whales swim, whales dive, whales float. They do not fall on people's heads."

"This one did" insisted Bungalow.

"All right George, all right, calm down" Harry came to Bungalow's defence "Obviously there is a bit more to this story. Where did this happen, Bung?"

"In Fgura" replied Bungalow.

"There, see" said George "Has anyone ever seen a whale in Fgura? I rest my case."

"Where in Fgura?" asked Harry patiently ignoring George's comment.

"Outside the fishmongers, you know the one with the big plastic whale hanging from the sign above the shop."

"I might have known" groaned George "There had to be a daft explanation, I suppose."

"It is not as daft as you may think" interjected Aris "All sorts of things have fallen from the sky especially after a tornado or a water spout. Fish have been sucked up over the sea and carried miles in the sky and then dropped over the land when the wind slows down. Well known fact. Even frogs."

"It must have been some storm to carry a whale" scoffed George "Anyway we are safe. It hardly ever rains in Malta so there is no fear of much dropping from the sky."

"And that is why I don't like flying" said Harry.

"Sorry Harry. You've lost me again" George was puzzled "What has a whale falling from the sky in Fgura got to do with you flying?"

"Flying is dangerous. Things drop from the sky" continued Harry. "Whales today, frogs tomorrow, planes next."

"That is just plain daft. No logic to it at all" moaned George "Anyway if you don't want to fly go by ship."

"Just as bad" said Harry.

"I've got to hear this "said George "You spent all those years in the navy and suddenly you're a landlubber! Go on, why can't you go by ship?"

"It was in the paper" explained Harry "That chap who hated flying so much he went on a ship."

 "What has that got to do with flying" George was about to tear his hair out– what little he had!

"A plane dropped out of the sky and hit the ship! It sank immediately" said Harry defiantly 'I rest my case."

"Pour me a Hop Leaf Ho. Quick as you can. I am beginning to lose my will to live" cried George.

"Anyway enough of all this chit chat, what's with all these decorations Do?" asked Aris "Is something special happening?"

Do smiled. She could hardly contain her excitement. "Tomorrow Mr Aris, my children are coming home" she said.

"Hey, that is good news" said Harry "Is it for good this time or just a visit?"

"No, it for good" said Ho smiling his happy smile. "They finish at University now so they soon work for you Mr Hally."

"Wonderful" said Pawlu "We must give them a welcome home party. What time will they get here?"

"Their flight get in at about eight tomorrow evening" said Ho "Rolletta will pick them up at the airport."

"Right lads" said Harry "On parade tomorrow night here at Ho's bar, eight o'clock. Don't be late."

Ho couldn't wait to see his twins again. They were grown up now and had both achieved distinctions in their chosen careers. Do had cooked a special meal and the bar had been decorated in true Chinese style in anticipation of their homecoming. When

Don finished his training he spent a couple of months working at the Bertazzoni family's Grand Hotel et de Milan and had flown to Liverpool to attend Din's graduation ceremony at the University of Liverpool. Din was pleased as she did not like flying just like Harry. They would return to Malta together.

The flight with Air Malta from Manchester was a good one and landed exactly on time at twenty minutes to eight. Don only had hand luggage but Din had two large cases. It was good that Don was with her to help.

As they emerged from the customs into the arrivals gate at Luqa Airport, they were met by a vast crowd of anxious faces of friends and relatives patiently awaiting their loved ones. Taxi drivers waved placards with names on them trying to identify their charges.

Lorretta was first to see the twins.

"Over here, Din. Hi Don" she shouted.

The twins smiled. The same smile that Ho made when he was happy. They trundled their bags through the crowd and Lorretta gave them both a welcoming hug.

"Let's get loaded" she said "And it is off to the Ho Chi Do Chi Bar. Let's go!"

Every seat had been taken in the bar as the villagers awaited the arrival of the children. Children! Some children! Don was over six feet tall and his sister only slightly shorter.

Lorretta parked her trusty Mercedes outside the bar ignoring the two yellow lines that had caused her Aunty Nora so much trouble in the past. This time she knew it would be OK as Constable

Alfred was much more understanding than the previous custodian of the Police station– Constable Spiteri.

It was some six years now since Constable Spiteri was involved in a contretemps with Harry and Nippy Nora. A minor collision between Harrys' Chevrolet and Nippy Nora's taxi had escalated into a major crime. Since he came to the village Constable Spiteri had been determined to catch the Nora/Barber gang as he called them but they were always one step ahead. Arresting them had become an obsession. The crash was his chance to get them. Unfortunately for him things did not work out as he hoped and instead of locking up the pair he ended up at St Lukes hospital where he was sectioned and spent the next three years at Mount Carmel mental home. He was medically discharged from the force and Alfred Ellul replaced him as the village constable.

But this was not the end for Spiteri. He still harboured desires to lock up Harry and Nora. No one understood why he was so vindictive least of all Harry. Nora had passed away while Spiteri was locked up but Harry was still at large. The ex constable now lived in Santa Lucia so it was just a short journey to Ħal–Luqa where he would go in disguise, complete with notebook and pencil to try to catch his adversary.

True to the discipline of his training he would note down the date, the time of day, names of any witnesses and any occurence that he felt may be used as evidence in his detremination to arrest Harry Barber. His attempts to keep under cover by dodging from doorway to doorway and hiding behind bins proved futile. As villagers passed by his various hideouts they would say

"Morning Constable. Nice day." His cover blown he would look for another hideout. He was on a mission. One that no one else cared about nor understood.

"Why don't you give up this crazy business?" asked Pawlu one day when he bumped into him near the pjazza "Harry's a good man. What's he ever done to harm you?"

"It is not a crazy business" answered Spiteri "And I am not crazy. I am as sane as the next man. I have a certificate to prove it."

No argument there. Better to let him go about his investigations. At least he was not harming anyone.

A great cheer went up as Din and Don entered the bar. Do rushed to embrace them with tears cascading down her cheeks. Ho smiled the happiest smile he had ever smiled and hugged his offspring with great joy. The entire bar now followed suit. Hugging, kissing, shaking hands, slapping backs.

"Give them some air" called George "here you two, come and sit over here." He gestured to a table in the middle of the bar which Do had laid out with finger food and nibbles. In the centre was magnificent cake on which she had carefully written in icing sugar *'Merħba, Din and Don'*.

Once again the Ho Chi Do Chi Bar rang out with the joyous sounds of celebration. Since the Chi's had arrived from Hong Kong and taken over the bar from old Joe, it seemed that nearly every week there had been a cause for one celebration or another. Today it was the turn of Din and Don. Needless to say the villagers had a million questions to ask the pair and the twins were pleased to answer every one of them.

"So my intrepid voyagers have returned" said Pawlu "We companions of the Ancient Order of Maltese Fishermen must stick together."

Din and Don embraced their 'Uncle' Pawlu.

"We have missed you all" said Don "Especially the fishing trips with Mario and Salvu."

Din glanced at Carmena and they both placed a finger alongside their nose, raised an eyebrow and moved the finger to seal their lips. The sign of the equally Ancient Order of the Great Guisseppa. The twins loved the intrigue that both Carmena and Pawlu had embroiled them in and who had committed them to the utmost secrecy.

The arrival of the Mayor Andrew and his ample wife Marella brought on another rousing cheer.

"Din and Don" greeted the Mayor "So you have come back to us. Safe and sound and ready to get going with your new careers. I guess you can't wait to get started."

"Enough of that Andrew" interrupted Marella. "They have only just landed. Let them have a drink and enjoy their friends. We can talk business tomorrow."

"You are right as always, my dear" Andrew never argued with his wife "Let me get you a drink. What will you have?"

The ample Marella spotted an empty chair next to an unsuspecting Harry. The fact that George had manoeuvred the seat into place did not occur to him. Any opportunity to bring

Harry in close proximity to the ample Marella and George could not resist.

"Harry" said the ample Marella "How are you? Isn't it wonderful to see these two lovely children again?"

Harry froze. How did she manage to get that close? The mischievous smile of George's face explained all. Harry glared at George. If looks could kill...

"I am very well" answered Harry "And yes it is wonderful to see them again" replied Harry rather stiffly trying to put some distance between his seat and that of the ample Marella.

It was not that Harry disliked the Mayoress. Far from it. He admired her very much. She was indeed a beautiful woman. Ample, it cannot be denied but nonetheless attractive because of it. It was just that Harry was not sure of her motives. He seemed to be the target of her intentions whenever they met.

Andrew had made his way over to the bar and signalled to Ho to strike the bar bell to get everyone's attention. Ho dutifully obeyed and the bar fell silent.

"My dear friends of Ħal-Luqa" started the Mayor, he knew how to milk a crowd "Today is a special day as two of our own have returned to be with us. They will soon be embarking on their new careers at the Greyhound Stadium in Ta Qali thanks to the wonderful generosity and dream of Harry Barber and his lovely sister Joan."

The bar erupted with a massive cheer and applause.

"Well done Don." "Love you Din." "Welcome home."

"So, let's raise our glasses and drink a toast to Din and Don...."

"To Din and Don" The twins blushed as the entire bar drank to their health.

"To Harry and Joan…"

Another resounding cheer.

"And to the entire village of Ħal–Luqa."

If the cheers had been any louder the roof would most certainly have blown off.

"Friends, today is the tenth of February and those of you who study our history will know it is the historic day of St Paul's Shipwreck. There was terrible storm and it spelt disaster for St Paul. 'D' for disaster. But, today is far from disaster. Today is the start of our future. 'D' for determination. 'D' for dedication'.  So I am going to call this day 'D Day' for Din and Don. Here's to the future."

As the roar of approval once again lifted the rafters the village Constable Alfred Ellul appeared in the doorway. He casually leaned against the door posts and smiled to himself as he observed the wonderful folk of his adopted village thoroughly enjoying themselves. It was approaching midnight and he knew he would have to quieten things down soon but…well there was no hurry.

"Constable Alfred" called Harry spotting him in the doorway "Come on in and have a drink. This is a special occasion." Harry went over to the reluctant policeman. In truth it was Harry's excuse to put some distance between himself and the ample Marella.

"Well, just a small one" said Alfred, after all he would soon be retired and be able to be a more regular patron of the Ho Chi Do Chi bar. No harm in a small toddy before bed time.

No one heard the telephone behind the bar. The noise had completely overwhelmed it. It was only when Do went behind to get some more glasses that she heard it.

"Hello" she answered "This is the Ho Chi Do Chi bar. Do speaking. How can I help you?"

"Do, this is Angus. Can you please get hold of Harry for me." said Angus. There was urgency in his voice.

"Of course" she replied "Hang on a minute."

Do rushed over to where Harry was talking to the Constable.

"Mr Harry" she said "There is call for you from Angus. It may be urgent."

Harry froze. Before his eyes he could see the word 'Disaster'.

He indicated to George to follow him to the 'phone.

"Hi Angus. What's up?"

"Wonderrful news, Harrry" Angus's tongue rolled out the news "Her Ladyship has delivered. Seven fine young pups."

Harry was speechless. This was the news he had been waiting for. But... there was a but!

"Are they OK" he asked "What do they look like?"

"What do you mean what do they look like?" laughed Angus.

"They look like seven plump, healthy puppies. They are already suckling from Her Ladyship. And she is as pleased as punch."

Harry was shaking partly with delight and partly with trepidation.

"Plump!" exploded Harry "Did he say plump?"

"Give me the phone" commanded George.

"Hi Angus. Great news. Harry is a bit shell shocked" explained George "How many dogs are there?"

"Not to worry George. He will get over it. There are five dogs and two bitches" said Angus "Listen I will stay here with Bung overnight just to keep an eye on them. Can you tell Joan for me?"

"No problem Angus. Well done mate."

George put the phone down and as he looked up he realised that the entire bar was now silent and all eyes were on him.

"Come on George" called Pawlu "What is the news?"

"Well it seems that Her Ladyship has blessed us with seven puppies. Five dogs and two bitches" announced George.

The loudest cheer of the night erupted. Everyone rushed to embrace and congratulate Harry and Joan.

"Dlinks on the house" announced Ho whose smile had become even broader.

Joan was overjoyed. Harry was mesmerised. No one, apart from George that is, knew his secret. George pulled Harry aside.

"What's up with you Harry" he said "You should be over the moon. This is what you wanted isn't it?"

"Yes. Of course it is" answered Harry "But don't you realise the date?"

"Yes. It is the tenth of February" said George.

"That's right" said Harry "And that is when we went to Dingli to find the non-existent intruder and when Bung left Fart on his own with Her Ladyship."

"Ah! Yes that may be a problem" said George.

"Precisely. The gestation period is sixty three days and today is exactly sixty three days" groaned Harry.

"But we don't know" said George "Maybe Lord Nodagan beat Fart to it. Let's not count our chickens before they're hatched."

"For crying out loud George. Before they're hatched! Too late. These are well and truly hatched."

"Calm down Harry" reassured George "We know nothing yet. It will probably be a couple of months before we will know for certain and even then it may be OK."

"Yes. That is some comfort" replied Harry sarcastically "We will most certainly know when seven Fart look-a-likes start running around."

"OK. OK. Look. There is nothing we can do about it now so let's go back into the bar and join in the celebrations as if nothing has happened."

Harry decided to put on a brave face and follow George's advice. After all what was done was done. He had to make the best of it.

"Harry where have you been?" the ample Marella called out to Harry as he re-entered the bar "You are a daddy now. Let me congratulate you."

She pulled Harry into her ample bosoms. For once Harry did not resist. He took advantage of this moment to enjoy the warmth of friendship and joyous darkness in the bosomness of the Lady Mayoress. For some reason he felt like a little boy again. A little boy who had lost his favourite toy and had sought solace in the comforting arms of his mother. Harry was about to cry. A mighty slap on his back brought him back to reality.

"*Prossit* Harry" said the Mayor "The plan is coming together.
Can't wait to see the dogs."

"Nor can I" said Harry but for a different reason.

"What will you name them?" asked Carmena.

"Er. Well, I have already chosen Thunder and Lightning, so I leave
to you to decide the names of the others" said Harry.

"What about Typhoon to keep the storm theme" said Aris.

"And Tornado" added No Lights.

"And Albert" said Pawlu.

"Albert!" exclaimed George "What has 'Albert' got to do with a
storm?"

"Yes, of course it has" replied Pawlu "Years ago when I was a boy
there was a terrible storm. In fact it was hurricane and it was
named Albert."

"Can't argue with that George" said Harry who was gradually
beginning to get back to his old self "Though I bet he will be the
first greyhound to be called Albert!"

"And as the bitches are the daughters of Her Ladyship they
should be named 'Princess' and 'Duchess'" said Carmena.

"Time for another toast I guess" said Ar s "Here's to Thunder,
Lightning, Typhoon, Tornado, Albert! and Duchess and Princess."

As the patrons raised their glasses for what seemed to be an
endless procession of toasts, Mario came rushing into the bar out
of breath but with a smile from ear to ear. Ho's ability to smile at
everything was catching on.

"Hey Mario. Where have you been?" saic Carmena "You have
missed all the fun."

"On the contrary" said Mario "We have been having some fun of our own. My lovely daughter Sandra has given birth to a beautiful bouncing boy."  Another cheer. Another toast.
"That is fantastic news" Carmena clapped her hands with joy. "Is Sandra OK? What does Tonio think about it? How much does he weigh? What will they call him?"
"Not Albert I hope" said George smiling.

It was all getting too much for Harry. The return of the twins, the birth of his puppies and now Sandra has had her baby. All on the tenth of February. Maybe Andrew was right. This was not a day of disaster. After all St Paul stayed in Malta for a long time after his shipwreck. Longer than he intended. He fell in love with the island and its people. Nothing had changed. Harry felt a lot happier at the thought. Maybe things would be OK in spite of his doubts.

As the villagers made their way home in the early hours old Guisseppa, awoken by the noise of the early morning revellers peered through her shutters in Triq San Gużepp whence she saw Harry, George and Aris arm in arm, hugging and holding each other up, meandering from side to side down the road to Triq San Ġorġ. What was it with men nowadays she wondered. The world is going crazy. She quickly closed the shutters, said ten Holy Mary's, crossed herself half a dozen times and reached for her Rosary. She would not sleep tonight. She had civilization to pray for.

# Easter Parade

"So when is Good Friday?" asked Aris.

"On Friday, if I remember correctly" replied George with his usual sarcasm.

"I know that you idiot. What I mean is what date is it? It changes every year. I just wondered when it would be this year. March or April" argued Aris.

"It is on the 25th March, Aris. Quite early this year" said Pawlu. He would know of course as he spent a lot of time with other volunteers preparing the various floats and statues for the Easter parade.

"Never understood why they keep changing the date" mused George "Christmas is fixed, Whitsun is fixed– why not Easter?"

"Apparently some  monks got together in about three hundred AD and decided that Easter should fall on the first Sunday after the first full moon following the spring equinox so it could happen at any time between March twenty second and April twenty fifth" explained Aris.

"Were they drunk at the time, these monks?" said George "Can't think of a more complicated way of calculating such an important event than this."

"I think that in those days the moon determined everything" added Aris.

"Fair enough but that still doesn't explain why it is not fixed" argued George.

"You have a point actually, George" added Harry "There must be records hidden somewhere in the Vatican detailing the exact date of the crucifixion. The Romans were always good at keeping records. Surely if they could look up the date it would solve the problem."

"The chances of getting anywhere near the secret records of the church are pretty remote" said George, cynical as ever.

"Even if they did find out I doubt if it would change anything" added Pawlu.

"I have always wondered what they had for supper that day" mused Aris.

"Good wholesome food I can tell you" said George "No fry ups. No fancy sauces. No processed foods."

" I bet they had rabbit with good fresh bread and lots of wine" said Harry.

"Did they have chocolate in those days?" asked Bungalow.

"Chocolate! Where did that come from?" asked George.

"Well it is tradition isn't it?" said Bung "Every Easter we have Easter eggs. Maybe Jesus liked chocolate and that is why we celebrate with chocolate eggs at Easter."

"Bung, old chap your explanation may be the answer that the whole world has been waiting for" said George "Well done, you may have solved a centuries old argument. Chocolate my friends. That is what Easter is all about."

"I'll drink to that" laughed Aris "But don't tell the Kappillan."

No doubt the Kappillan would have despaired if he had heard Bungalow's explanation, but he was too involved for the preparations for the Good Friday procession. Like many other towns and villages in Malta, Good Friday was a major part of the church's annual celebrations. Ħal-Luqa had a reputation for being one of the best. Many hours of preparation went into the event. The statues, the floats, the costumes all had to be prepared, renovated and cleaned. All the work was completed by volunteers as it was a labour of love.

On the Thursday following Palm Sunday, a cohort of Roman soldiers would march through the village streets which were deserted. Night had already fallen and the streets were lit with dim, yellow coloured lights which gave off a sinister glow. The squadron was led by the drummers who beat muffled drums. The *tum, tum, tumpity tum* resounded off the walls of the houses. The villagers peered from being their shutters not daring to venture out. The atmosphere of doom, of impending disaster was everywhere. It was if the village had receded into the past.

The soldiers themselves were immaculate in their uniforms with highly polished helmets and silver breast plates. Their leather sandals precisely laced. The participants in this pageant had made every effort to retain the authenticity of the original. The breast plates alone, worn by the soldiers were worth as much as ten thousand euros. Such was the commitment and enthusiasm of the particpants. Julius Caesar would have been proud of them. They made their way through the village along Triq San Ġorġ, up to Triq Dun Pawl and to the church where a fanfare of trumpets warned the village of their presence. Even after all these years, the presence of the drummers struck fear into the hearts of the villagers.

The main parade would be on Good Friday and would start at seven p.m. when there was still daylight. The first warning of the procession would be earlier when the immaculately dressed soldiers would blast a fanfare in front of the church and would then head up a procession of drummers and soldiers who would march through the village returning to the church at exactly seven o'clock when the main procession would emerge from the main doors of the chuch.

In preparation for the parade the good villagers of Ħal-Luqa would open their doors and put chairs onto the pavement where they would sit with their families and chat with passersby.  The wine would flow and *pastizzi* and *ħobż u żejt* would be offered in ample proportions.

Harry had invited Joan and Angus to join him at his house in Triq San Ġorġ to watch the parade. George and Aris had also turned up with a good supply of wine needless to say. The doom and gloom of Thursday night had turned into joy and elation even though the day was one of mourning.

As the church bells which had been muffled in respect for the occasion, clappity clapped the time, so the procession started. An ear shattering fanfare from the Roman trumpeters heralded the start of the celebrations.The first figure to appear was that of a young lad clad in long white robes and carrying a shepherd's rod. Over the next two hours a steady stream of characters from both the old and new Testament made their way out of the main church doors. It was a wonder of organisation that so many people with all their paraphernalia could have been accommodated inside. But it was a well rehearsed routine and the elders of the village had done it all before.

It seemed like the whole village had dressed up as characters from the good book led by Noah and his sons Shem, Ham and Jepath. Children from the village herded their animals two by two, chickens, geese, rabbits, dogs, donkeys, even greenfinches,canaries and budgies.

The children dressed in the clothes of the time. Some carrying their hamsters, pigeons and pet mice. The procession would advance slowly taking perhaps twenty paces and then stopping allowing the viewing crowds to enjoy the costumes that the participants had spent many hours meticulously making.

A finely robed Pharaoh with his beautiful wife and an entourage of servants waving palms strode majestically from the pjażża. He was followed by King Solomon and his wife and a few steps behind the very naughty Queen of Sheba. And so on through all the characters of the bible. The twelve apostles walked together. St Peter, St Thomas, all the Saints and of course Judas who, still clutching his pieces of silver, fended off the boos of the crowd. The rooster was carried by a young boy. Pontius Pilate carefully guarded by his entourage walked majestically by, paying little heed to the disapproval of the crowd. At the rear of the procession was the Ark of the Covenant carried on nine foot staves by four strong men dressed in the robes of Levi priests. Behind it came the Kappillan accompanied by his assistant priests, the magnificent float of the *Redentur* and finally the marching band of the Stella Band Club.

In Triq San Ġorġ Harry's party were well into their third bottle of wine. The procession had already reached them. It was still March and now that the winter sun had gone down the evening was getting colder. Some of the children had only flimsy costumes and Joan feared that they would all catch pneumonia. She need not have worried. The Maltese mothers knew how to protect their offspring and had made sure they had warm clothes beneath the costumes. As the children passed by, the villagers made sure they were well supplied with sweets and warm drinks.

Most of the procession had now passed when round the corner came four strong lads carrying the Ark of the Covenant. They stopped outside Harry's house. Harry handed out *pastizzi* and wine to the grateful guardians of the Ark.

As they raised the Ark to continue on their way one of the staves that supported it snapped and the box fell to the road. Disaster. The pole that they had used to carry the Ark was broken in half. It could not be repaired.

The Kappillan who was further down the road saw what had happened and came running. He surveyed the damage and making the sign of the cross said "It's no good we can't go any further with it. We will have to leave it in the road."
"Excuse me, Father" said Harry coming to the rescue "I think it would be safer if I put it in my front room. At least if it rains it will not get damaged."
"Harry, you are our saviour" said the priest "Thank you so much. We will collect it in the morning."
   The four lads lifted the Ark which was very heavy and placed it in the centre of Harry's front room. Their journey was over. The procession continued on its way as if nothing had happened.
"Well now" said George "We have something of a dilemma here, haven't we?"
"What are you scheming now George" asked Aris.
"You realise Mr Harold Barber, that you are now the custodian of the Ark of the Covenant" explained George.
"Yes, so what?" answered Harry.
"For the last four thousand years the world has been desperate to know what it contains. It has been a mystery that has never been resolved" continued George "You now have the opportunity to solve that mystery. Take a peek inside Harry. You will be famous when you reveal the truth."
"Don't be daft, George. It is a replica. Nothing inside" replied Harry.

"How do you know?" retorted George "For all we know it might be the real thing. It might contain the tablets that Moses brought down from Mount Horeb."

Aris, Angus and Joan were doubled up with laughter.

"As Michael Miles used to say '*Open the Box*'."

George issued the  command pointing at the Ark. George could not keep a straight face any  longer. He broke out laughing at Harry's serious face.

"Stop winding me up George. You're at it again" said Harry "I try to do a favour for the parish and all you can do is take the micky out of me."

"But this is your chance Harry" continued George "They might make you the next Pope. Pope Harold the First, no less."

"That's enough George" said Joan laughing "Leave my brother alone."

"You're right" said George "Sorry mate. Couldn't resist it. But just imagine if it was true. Wow! Luqa would surely be on the map then."

"You are incorrigible George" said Joan "Come on, drink up, let's go up to the square to see the end of the parade."

With that they set off with the rest of the village to see the end of another successful Good Friday procession.

The secrets of the Ark were safe for another year. A sigh of relief emitted from the Vatican.

# Welcome to our World

Harry spread a generous layer of marmalade on his toast as he had done since he was a boy. A creature of habit, his breakfast had not changed even though his loyal housekeeper Lucia had tried to entice him with bacon and eggs even a sausage or two. He was set in his ways. Two shredded wheat followed by two slices of toast made with Maltese bread. He toasted the bread under the grill as his electric toaster could not take the thick slice that he cut off the loaf. This would all be washed down with a large mug of strong tea, so strong that you could stand up a spoon in it. *Kikkra te bil-ħalib u nofs kuċċarina żokkor.* A cup of tea with half a spoon of sugar. How many times had Lucia heard him say that!

She had looked after Harry for a good many years now and knew his ways inside out. Harry was an easy man to please as all he wanted was a peaceful life with no complications. She lived in Triq Il-Ġdida which was only one street away and their purely platonic relationship had worked well for them both.

Lucia had never married and had spent most of her life caring for her mother who was a victim of severe diabetes which had affected her sight. To make ends meet she had accepted Harry's offer to be his housekeeper and when her mother died she continued with her work for Harry. She took great pride in her work and kept Harry's house immaculately clean. The one thing that did annoy her was when Harry decided to paint his fridge bright yellow! He had two fridges. The white one for food and the yellow one for beer.

"Fridges are for food, Harry" she complained "Not beer."

"But beer *is* food" insisted Harry laughing. Why was it that women could never understand the concept!

"But why paint the fridge?"asked Lucia.

"In case there is a power cut at night" explained Harry as if it was a daft question.

"What difference will that make?" she replied puzzled.

"The paint is luminous. It will shine in the dark so I will waste no time opening the wrong fridge" Harry said satisfied that his explanation made sense.

"*Stupidu*" said Lucia raising her eyes to the heavens.

Harry glanced at the calendar that was attached to the front of the yellow fridge.

"Do you know what day it is Lucia?" asked Harry.

"Yes it is Tuesday" she replied.

"I know, but do you know what is special about it?"

"Yes. It is raining" she replied wondering what Harry was leading up to.

"Exactly" said Harry taking a gulp of his third cup of tea "Tradition."

"Sorry  Harry, you confuse me. What has raining got to do with tradition?" she asked, patiently playing along with Harry's ramblings. She was used to him by now!

"Ah! You see, it is tradition. There was  an old man who lived in Mqabba. He was the oldest man in the village. No-one knew how old he was" explained Harry "But he was also the wisest. You see he said that on April 14th every year there would be a rain storm and that would be the end of winter. There would be no more rain until the 8th September. From today the temperature will rise and we can start wearing our shorts again."

He was right. Every year on the 14th April it rains. And this year was no different.

"Is that so"said Lucia "If it makes you happy to believe the ramblings of some old man from Mqabba then that is up to you. Me, I listen to the weather forecast."

"Don't under estimate folk lore" said Harry wagging his finger "Our forefathers knew a thing or two especially about the weather. We should listen to them."

"Well as long as the weather is good for Sunday that is all that matters" said Lucia.

"Why, what is happening on Sunday?" asked Harry.

"Surely you have not forgotten!" said Lucia "It is the christening of Sandra's baby."

"Oh my goodness. I had forgotten" said Harry "How could I forget. And I am one of the God fathers."

The baby was two months old now. Mario and Carmen, Tonio's parents were overjoyed with their grandson. He was truly their bundle of joy. Like all doting grand mothers, Carmen could not wait to cuddle him.When the baby was a month  old Carmen had set about making the christening gown. Carmen was a skilled seamstress and Sandra had asked her to make the gown from her wedding dress.

 Another tradition!

The finished dress was magnificent. Carmen had done her daughter proud. When Sandra's father Salvu, saw it he was overcome with emotion. His daughter had given him a  fine grandson and he was the proudest man in the village. He told everyone he met that he was a *Nannu.* The christening was arranged for Sunday the nineteenth. Most of the village was invited but since Salvu and Mario were so well  known and liked, no doubt even those who were not invited would turn up. After all the church is for everyone! The celebrants would revert to the Ho Chi Do Chi Bar afterwards.

The proud parents had decided not to reveal the name they had chosen for the baby until the actual ceremony. Naturally there was much speculation among the ladies of the village. The

favourite was Andrew of course, out of respect for the patron
Saint of the village.

Tradition!

Others argued that as Sandra and Tonio were a modern couple
they would choose something more up to date, but the odds
favoured a name from traditional jazz. All would be revealed on
Sunday.

Just as Harry had predicted and the old man of Mqabba had
foretold, Sunday was a beautiful day. No rain. The streets that
had been drenched on Tuesday were now dry as a bone which
was just as well as the family had decided to walk to the church
rather than take cars as parking was a major problem nowadays.

The service would take place at four in the afternoon so that
everyone would have plenty of time to prepare. This was an
opportunity for the ladies to put on their best frocks while the
men dug out their black suits which only saw the light of day at
christenings, weddings and funerals.

The Marozzi family set off from their house in Triq Tarxien at
fifteen minutes to four. They must not be late for what would be
one of the most important days in the baby's life. Not that he
knew anything about it. He was quite happy as Sandra had had
the foresight to give him a good feed in the hope that he would
sleep through the ceremony. Good thinking. As they walked to
the church they were cheered on with best wishes from the
villagers stopping every few steps as the ladies asked to have a
peep at the new arrival. Salvu feared they would be late but it
really didn't matter. The baby had his whole life ahead of him. He

was in no hurry. Why rush! A full stomach, a warm gown in the comfort of his mother's arms,all he wanted now was to sleep.

The church was full. Sandra and Tonio were very popular in the village. The villagers of Ħal-Luqa had come to welcome the baby into their village and into their faith.
Tradition.

Harry, George and Aris had taken their seats in the front row with the family. Harry was to be one of the God fathers along with Johnny Azzopardi from the band and Sandra's Aunty Carmena and Lorretta the taxi driver as God Mothers. She had chosen Lorretta besause she was the niece of Nippy Nora who had died several years ago and who had been a special friend of hers when she was a girl.

"Never thought I would see you inside a church, George" said Harry smiling to himself. George had a very cynical opinion about religion which he  would expound to anyone who would listen. Not that anyone did!

"The whole thing is a scam" he would say "How anyone could fall for such a load of nonsense is beyond me."

"I see" said Harry "So millions of people over the centuries have been wrong and you, Oh wise one, is the only one who knows the truth! Is that right?"

"Right" answered George "How anyone could believe the Joseph and Mary yarn is crackers. If that happened today they would be laughed at. 'Oh! Joseph I am pregnant and it isn't yours but this spirit blessed me with it'. Come on pull the other one."

"You're a cynical old misery George" said Harry.

"Maybe but I will say no more" answered George supping his pint.

 "And for that I thank God" said Harry "Now shut up and enjoy the ceremony."

George muttered under his breath.  Why was it no one took any notice of him! He had developed his theories about religion and politics during his time in the navy.There are times in service life when the crew are bored stiff and conversation often turns to religion, origin of the human race and the universe. Many theories abound. George loved to expound on them even though he did not believe in them.  He just enjoyed the banter and the argument that followed. The truth was he liked winding people up and it was easy to get Harry going.

The christening party took their seats at the front of the church. There were two other couples celebrating the birth of their little ones. For the moment all three babies were asleep. The church bells chimed four o'clock and precisely on time the Kappillan appeared. The baptism of new life was one of the Kappillan's favourite duties. Welcoming a new life into the world is always a happy occasion when families and friends come together to share their joy.

The ceremony went well. The babies slept. The parents and God parents all performed their duties correctly and the congregation behaved as a congregation should. Even George behaved himself. The moment during the ceremony when the babies would be named had come. All ears were concentrated on what the Kappillan would say. As he came to the part in the ceremony where he named the baby he mischieviously hesitated

knowing that the entire congregation were on the edge of their seats waiting to hear the chosen names  *"Fl-isem ta-Missier Iben u l-Ispirtu s-Santu, jien ħaddimkom ...pause...more pause...Louis Andrew Marozzi..."* His next words were drowned in a great sigh of approval from the congregation. Louis was obviously chosen out of respect for the great  Louis Armstrong,Tonio's jazz hero and  Andrew for the patron Saint of Ħal-Luqa.
"Well done Tonio" called Harry "With names like that he will go far."

   With the ceremony over the ladies crowded around Sandra to congratulate her and to get a closer view of the young Louis Andrew. There  were tears in Carmen's eyes as the proud Grand Mother took the baby from his mother's arms. It was her turn to have a cuddle.

   The men did what all men do on such occasions. They shook Tonio's hand, slapped him on the back and whisked him off to the bar to wet the baby's head.

   As she had done so many times before, Do with the expert help of Don had prepared a magnificent buffet for the baby's special day. Apart from the standard finger foods and the mandatory sausage rolls- in case Fart made an appearance- she had prepared some delicious delicacies of pastries with lobster and crab. Once again the Ho Chi Do Chi bar resounded with the excited chatter of its patrons. Nothing motivated a village more than the arrival of a baby. Today was no exception. The ladies discussed who he looked like while the men argued about which football team he would support. He was in good company.

Once everyone had attended to their stomachs and had downed a few drinks, it was time for the formal photos. Lorretta was a keen photographer and her services were called upon to compose the family album. She was aided by Johnny Azzopardi the drummer from Tonio's band.

"Do I spy a romance developing here" whispered Carmena clutching her black plastic handbag "I think there may be more celebrations to come."

The photo session complete Sandra decided it was time to get the little one home for another feed and more sleep!

"You know, I wonder why we bother to grow up sometimes" said George "Look at him. He's got it  made. Food every four hours, drink on demand and then sleep. What more could a man want?"

"Yes, I can just see it now" laughed Harry "George sitting in the corner with a great big dummy in his mouth. At least we will get some peace and quiet."

"Peace and quiet!" exclaimed Carmena "There speaks a man who has a never raised a child. Any mother will tell you them last thing you will get is peace and quiet. Am I right, Do."

"Ah so" said Do "Waking up in the middle of the night for his feed when you are exhausted. Changing nappies. I remember it all well."

"Now there's a sight I would not want to see" said Harry "Changing George's nappies. I  doubt if you  will get any volunteers for that chore!"

Everyone was convulsed with laughter at the thought. George was beginning to wish he had kept his mouth shut.

"Never mind George" said Carmena "Your Aunty Carmena will change your nappy for you. I will stand you in the back yard and squirt the hosepipe all over you. That should do the trick."

The very thought of George being hosed down with a great big dummy in his mouth brought on another wave of hysterical laughter.

" OK, OK" George held his hands in the air "I surrender. You've had your fun. I'll just sit here in the corner and drink my beer and leave the babies to you lot."

"At last the man is talking sense" remarked Harry "Give him a drink Ho. And give him a straw in case he spills it."

"What George spill his beer!" joked Aris "That'll be the day."

George really was in the firing line. He took it in good part especially when Mario gave him one of Louis' dummies to suck.

The evening had drawn to a close. Everyone had enjoyed a great time albeit at the expense of George. But then this was Ħal-Luqa. No-one held a grudge. Everything was done and said with good humour. Louis Andrew had been formally received by the villagers and his head had been well and truly wetted.

All he had to do now was to grow up and what better place to do so than in Ħal-Luqa. He would be well cared for although it is unlikely that he could rely on George for a nappy change!

# Harry buys a camera

The early morning intoxicating aroma of freshly baked bread that permeated through the village called Harry to the bakery in Triq San Gużepp. The traditional round Maltese loaf once tasted could never again be resisted. The warm loaf with its hard crust and deliciously fibrous soft centre had been the staple diet of the Maltese for centuries. None the least during the second World War when the island faced starvation. The bread makers of Qormi had worked overtime to feed the population while they awaited the arrival of the Santa Maria convoy. The same ovens and the same techniques that saved the nation were still used to this day.

"Stocking up with your *ħobż*, I see" greeted Aris who was also on a similar mission.

"Of course" answered Harry "Can't get through the day without it. I am glad I bumped into you Aris. You see I wanted some advice."

"Only too pleased to oblige if I can. What's up?" said Aris.

"I was thinking of buying a camera to record the life of the dogs but I don't know where to start" he continued "You were a photographer when you were in the RAF weren't you? Can you come to Valletta with me to buy one?"

"Well strictly speaking I wasn't a photographer I was an interpreter of photographs" corrected Aris "Although I do remember on one occasion doing a job for the photo department at RAF Luqa."

"Oh! What was that?" asked Harry.

"They wanted some ID pictures of the civilian staff at the USAF Wheelus base in Tripoli and couldn't find anyone to do it. So I volunteered. Big mistake. I should have known. Never volunteer!" Aris smiled to himself.

"So what went wrong?" asked Harry intrigued.

"Didn't exactly go wrong but as I had to take the shots on an MPP plate camera, I thought I would save the RAF  some money and put eight people in each shot instead of just one. I could then do the individual pics in the darkroom" explained Aris.

"The problem was that  all the workers wore caps which they had to remove for the photo. Well that was OK but when I came to print I had a massive problem."

"No, not with you. What was the problem?"

"The workers all worked outside so their faces were heavily sunburnt. They wore the caps to protect their heads. This meant that most of them were bald and when they took off their caps their heads were white from the eyebrows up! So when I went to print I had some two hundred men whose faces stopped at their eyebrows and the tops of their heads were totally missing!" Harry started to laugh.

"It wasn't funny. I got a right telling off" groaned Aris "Had to go back and do it all over again. Probably cost the RAF a fortune. The CO was puce with anger especially as he had to go cap in hand to explain to the USAF Commander what had happened."

"So did you get it sorted?" sked Harry still chuckling to himself.

"Yes. No problem. In fact the yanks were great. Never ate so much food in all my life. I did think about mucking  it up again so I could go back. Thought better of it though. Anyway I am happy to come with you. When do you want to go?"

"Later this morning. OK?" said Harry,

"No problem. Let me get my bread and then I will meet you at the bus stop. I've been wanting to see what they have done to the entrance to Valletta anyway" smiled Aris

The journey to Valletta only took twenty minutes and as Harry and Aris alighted opposite the Phoenicia Hotel they were somewhat taken aback. It had been a long time since either of them had been to *Il–Belt–* the capital. What confronted them was a building site! Boarding had been erected around the Triton Fountain. All the buses had been moved to St James ditch. The whole area seemed to be chaotic mix of people, buses, taxis, cranes and builders vehicles. The street traders were still there selling their souvenirs and cakes, pastiżżi, cheese rolls and piżżas. The hustle and bustle was even more intense than Harry remembered.

"What the heck is going on?" he asked Aris.

"Don't ask me" answered Aris "Looks like World War Two all over again. Let's get closer."

As they passed the RAF monument Aris stopped and saluted it dutifully. Tradition and respect still coursed through his veins.They ploughed their way through the crowds and reaching the bridge they looked with disbelief as they viewed the new entrance to the city.

"Where's it gone?" said Harry "What have they done?"

"This is not Valletta" said Aris "It's supposed to be a fortress city. Where is the gateway?"

"But it is ...I don't know what to say. It is bland. No character at all" cried Harry "It is more like the pyramids. An entrance to Cairo not Valletta."

"I wonder what they have done to the Opera House?" said Aris fearing the worst "Let's see."

They made their way over the bridge and into the square where they viewed the new parliament building. Harry was dumbstruck.

"Oh! Aris. What the...." said Harry.

"Well! It is certainly different" said Aris as he viewed Renzo Piano's design.

"Yes but..." said Harry lost for words.

"Actually" continued Aris "I think it is rather magnificent. Totally inappropriate of course for a Baroque city but nevertheless quite attractive."

"It is not Valletta" said Harry "Or at least not the Valletta that I remember and love. This was supposed to be a city built by gentlemen for gentlemen – '*Citta' Umilissima'*. La Valette must be turning in his grave. And look at the Opera House. It is not one thing or another. What a lost opportunity!"

"All those steps are a bit intimidating I must admit. Can't see me using them. Knees are not up to it" lamented Aris.

"Valletta is supposed to be a fortress city" continued Harry "But they've removed the gate so it has lost its fortifications! No. Sorry, I don't like it."

"I need a drink" said Harry "Come on. Let's see if Prego's is still there."

   They set off down South Street and where relieved to find the cafe that they used to visit was still there and still the same. Harry was particularly pleased to discover that his old friend Giovanni still worked there.

*"Tnejn cappuċino, jekk jogħġbok"* said Harry stretching his Maltese vocabulary to its limit "Good to see you Gianni. How are you these days? Still working?"

"Harry, my good friend" said Gianni shaking Harry's hand warmly "Of course I am still working. What else I do?"

"I thought you would have put your feet up by now" replied Harry "Or retired on your yacht to Sorrento or somewhere."

"Yacht! Ha! Some hopes" laughed Gianni "On my pension? No I could stay at home I suppose and drink my  coffee, read the paper and stare at the walls or I can come here have a coffee, read the paper and meet some very nice people. What would you do?"

"Good on you Gianni" said Harry "Long may you do it."

   Gianni had worked at the cafe for as long as Harry could remember and was considered to be part of the fittings.

"See Aris, not everything changes, thank goodness" said Harry sipping his coffee.

"Well I guess everything changes with time" said Aris.

"Why?" said Harry.

"Its progress I guess. Can't stand still can you?" he went on "Be a bit boring if nothing ever changed."

"Change OK, but not change for change sake and certainly not for the worse" replied Harry who seemed to be getting worked up about the new buildings "I never liked it when they changed the name Kingsway to Republic Street. Kingsway had a regal tone to it. Stability, honour, respectability. Republic is, er, I don't know, sinister, grey, dictatorial."

"Well. We have to live with it, that is for sure" said Aris" so drink up and let's find this camera for you."

A traipse around the many camera shops in Valletta brought Harry no nearer to a solution as to what to buy.

"Come on Aris" jibed Harry "I thought you were going to advise me."

"Sorry Harry, but it is all different now from what I know of photography" groaned Aris "When I was in it the cameras we all aspired to were Rolleiflexes and Leicas.  But all that has gone now with digital photography."

"See, change is not always appreciated is it?" laughed Harry.

"Well it was so sudden. One minute we had films that took thirty six pictures next it was a small piece of plastic that took a thousand shots" explained Aris " But the bit I don't like is that when  we had film, the photographer was a mixture of an artist and a technician.  He had to make every shot count. Now he just fires away in the hope that one shot will be acceptable. The camera does the work not the photographer."

"So what is wrong with that?" asked Harry.

"Nothing I suppose except the taking of pictures, processing and printing was a hobby and one that gave great satisfaction" continued Aris "But now it is point and shoot and little thought put into it. Shame really."

"Well that doesn't help me" said Harry.

"You know you can take quite good pics with your mobile 'phone, don't you?" said Aris

"Really?" said Harry "But I don't use a mobile. Can't understand them."

"Then there is no hope for you" Aris concluded.

In the end Harry bought a compact Nikon camera which would suit his needs admirably even though he would probably never use all the features that it offered.

"Come on then" said Harry "Let's go home and get the Chevvy, we can pick up George and go and see the dogs."

As they  weaved their way back through the congested and thriving Merchants Street into Republic Street, Harry took a last glance at the new parliament building, shook his head in disgust and decided it would be a long time before he visited Valletta again.

# The truth is out!

The road to the kennels at Dingli was narrow and full of pot holes so Harry drove slowly so as not to damage his pride and joy. He had inherited the Chevrolet Impala from Idaho Joe who had left it in Harry's safe hands when he went to Australia. The car was still in very good condition partly due to Harry's conscientious care of the vehicle and partly because of the Maltese climate. In spite of being in the middle of a salty sea, cars did not seem to rust. There were still cars, trucks even buses that were sixty, seventy years old driving around. No doubt they had had many engines and gear boxes over the years but the original chassis was still there.Due in some cases to the innate attitude of the Maltese in that they would never throw anything away. They would get the maximum life out of everything and refused to waste any part. The many years of siege conditions and deprivation had inbred this way of life.

It was late afternoon as the Chevvy pulled into the farm. Bungalow, Pawlu, Angus and Joe were already there working with the dogs who were now about six months old.

"Hi guys" called Harry "How is everything?" not wanting an answer. The greyhounds all ran over to greet the arrivals.

"They are looking very fit" said George "You are doing a grand job by the looks of it, Angus old chap."

"Aye" said Angus "They are coming on a trreat. No worrrries."

"When can we start their race training Angus?" asked Harry.

"Och, not for a while yet Harry" replied Angus "Still a wee bit young. Maybe when they are a year old. Next February perhaps they should be ready."

"That long" mused Harry.

"Aye, but Harry, There is something I wanted to mention" said Angus in a low conspiratorial voice.

Harry feared the worst.

"What's that Angus?" asked Harry.

"Well, now the pups are growing up, I can't help noticing that they are a bit different from normal greyhounds."

"Oh! Why so?" said Harry fully knowing what was coming next.

"Take a close look, mate" Idaho added.

"No. What do you mean?" Harry kept up the act but glanced sideways to George who was straight-faced.

"Well they have greyhound heads admittedly but they are very hairy and rather plump around the middle" said Angus "not the streamlined speed machines that you would expect of a pure bred greyhound."

"Mmm. Maybe you're right but as they get older they will slim down won't they?" asked Harry trying to convince himself.

"Aye. They might but then they might also get fatter" said Angus "If you look at Lord Nodagan and Her Ladyship you could be excused for thinking they were not the parents."

George pulled Harry aside.

"I think we have to come clean Harry" he said "Our worst suspicions seem to have come true. I think it is time to let them in on your secret."

Harry pondered for a minute then turning to Angus and Idaho said "Angus, Joe, listen, I have to explain something" he paused to get his thoughts together.

"You remember that time when Bungalow thought we had an intruder and George and I came out to help him?"

"Aye, it was last December. Some fellow named Roger if I remember correctly" said Angus.

"Well, unbeknown to us at the time, Bung had let Fart enter the dogs' enclosure and it looks like he had his wicked way with Her Ladyship."

"Oh No!" exclaimed Joe.

"The consequence is running around in front of you" said George gesturing towards the dogs "Take a close look.These wonderful specimens are the offspring of Fart. They are Farthounds."

"This is disastrous" said Angus "What can we do? We can't race them as thoroughbreds now.Their pedigree has been violated."

"Hold on a sec mate" said Joe "I had a strange feeling about this all along. But we can't let a little thing like this stop us. There must be a way of getting around it. Let's think about it before we do anything."

"What can we do?" said Harry who was now in desperation as he saw all that he had dreamed of fading away. "You can see from a mile off that these are not genuine greyhounds!  We don't stand a chance."

"Yeah. OK. But what if we did a bit of jigging around" said Joe scheming away.

"Bit late for that. Someone should have jigged around with Fart a long time ago and then this disaster would not have happened" said Harry angrily.

"Now that's unfair Harry" said Joe "He was only answering the call of nature. Not his fault" Joe tried to calm the situation.

"Listen we can keep the dogs on strict diet. Always put blankets on them when we walk them so strangers won't realise. And we can give them regular hair cuts to make them look more like greyhounds. What do you think?"

"I think we have no choice if we want to go ahead" said George.

"But what if someone finds out?" said Harry.

"Who's going to find out?" said Joe "I won't tell anyone and all of us can swear to keep it secret. What's the problem?"

"You're a rogue Idaho" said Harry still not convinced but warming to the idea.

"I think you may be on to something Joe" added Aris "But apart from what they look like with Fart as a father do you think they will be able to run?"

"Well that's easily solved" said George smiling "If you have ever seen Fart run when he has had a whiff of a hot sausage then I would defy any greyhound to keep up with him! No, no problems there I reckon."

Everyone nodded in agreement.

"Ok" said George "Let us all, here and now swear an oath of secrecy."

"I'll go along with that" said Pawlu who could see all his hard work building the kennels coming to nothing.

George continued "Right. Form a circle. Raise your right hands and put your left hand on each other's" he commanded.  With sombre faces they did as he instructed.

"Now say after me..." He cleared his throat.

"I ...say your name... promise and swear that I will never reveal and always conceal the parentage of the dogs of the Harry Barber Kennels, namely Thunder, Lightning, Typhoon, Tornado, Albert, Duchess and  Princess to anyone in the world upon the certain penalty that if I do I will be banned from the Ho Chi Do CHi Bar forever. So help me God."

The oath taken they bounced their hands three times and the deal was done.

"Right, so that is it" said George "We never mention this again. We go on as if Lord Nodagan is the sire. Agreed?"

They all nodded.

"Cheer up Harry, it will be all right. You'll see" said Aris "Now where's that camera. Let's get some pics in the album."

# Is-Senna It-Tajba

"I've seen some right miserable faces in my time but tonight Harry, you take the biscuit" said George.  "What's the matter with you man? It's New Years Eve. You should be happy, singing your head off and drunk. This is not like you."

"I'm OK George. Got a few things on my mind. That's all" said Harry.

"So let's get them off your mind. You're among friends here. Everything will be fine" added Aris "What's troubling you? Is it the dogs?"

"What else?" answered Harry "I know they are coming on fine and Joe and Angus are doing  a great job but I can't help thinking it is all going to go wrong. Someone is bound to ask questions when they see them."

"Rubbish man" said Joe "I've never seen such fine specimens. When Angus has finished training them they will be the lean, mean speed machines that you wanted."

"I hope so" said Harry still not convinced.

"Anyway, how is the photography going? I haven't seen any pictures yet" said Aris.

"Oh! I am good at taking pictures all right, Aris" said Harry "Trouble is they are all in the camera and I don't know how to get them out."

"It's easy. Just transfer into your computer and print them off" explained Aris.

"But I haven't got a computer. You said it would be easy but it all seems too complicated now with this digital stuff" complained Harry "I used to take my roll of film into the chemist and next day I could pick up thirty six pictures to show to my friends and put in an album."

"You're not really with it are you Harry?" laughed Aris "Not quite ready for the twenty first Century I guess."

"I'm only just getting the hang of the twentieth let alone this one" moaned Harry "Why is everyone in such a hurry? Everything has to be immediate. I blame it on instant coffee."

"I'll drink to that" said George who was always ready to drink to anything for that matter.

"Give me the camera Harry. I will sort it for you" said Aris.

"You're a gent, Aris" said Harry "Appreciate your help. Anyway you're right George, it is New Year's Eve and I need to cheer up. Has Ho got anything arranged for tonight or is it the traditional booze up?"

"Hey, Ho" George called to Ho who was busy behind the bar "What's on the agenda for tonight? Anything special?"

"Of course" replied Ho "I think you forget. This is Constable Afled rast shift. Tonight he will letire. We cereblate."

"I'd completely forgotten" said Harry disgusted with himself for not remembering "What's the time Aris?"

"Seven. Might be a bit later. My watch is a bit slow sometimes. Must get a new second hand for it" answered Aris.

"You are unbelieveable Aris" said George "You can buy a good watch at the *monte* for a couple of pounds. Why struggle with that one? It only tells you the hour."

"My father gave it to me when I was a boy" answered Aris "It has sentimental value. Anyway the church bells tell us the time every fifteen minutes. I don't really need a watch."

Aris was right of course and the bells had just rang for a quarter to eight.

"Right, well there's the bells now and Alfred signs off at eight so somehow we need to get him to come straight here" said Harry.

"Harry, Harry, calm down man" said Pawlu "It is all in hand. I had a word with some of his old colleagues and they are coming over at eight thirty to give him a surprise and a send off. His Inspector is meeting Alfred at eight and bringing him here for an official drink."

"You've been busy Pawlu" said George "Well done."

"Not all down to me" said Pawlu "Ho and Do have been a great help. The plan is that when Alfred comes in with his boss we all ignore him and then as his pals arrive some of the musicians from the Police band will suddenly appear in the bar and give him a resounding send off."

There was a buzz of anticipation as the patrons of the Ho Chi Do Chi Bar awaited the arrival of the unsuspecting constable and his Inspector. Harry noticed that the curtains around the stage had been closed tight.

"Is Tonio's band not playing tonight, Ho?" asked Harry "Special occasion, I thought we would have some music."

"I can answer that Harry" said Mario "He and Sandra have decided to stay at home with their children so me and Carmen and her Dad, Salvu, can see the New Year in. No baby sitting tonight."

"Fair enough" said Harry.

George looked at his watch. It was five past eight, they would be here soon.

"Fill your glasses everyone" he called "They are on their way. Remember, ignore them when they come in."

Ho quickly made sure everyone had their drink and just in time as Alfred and the Inspector entered. No-one looked up. They all carried on with their conversations. Not that Alfred was expecting anything but he was a little perturbed that Harry and George had not acknowledged him. After all they knew this was his last duty.

"What are you having Alfred" asked the Inspector.

"My usual Blue Label please" he replied "I think Harry and I keep Farsons in business with Blue sales."
Just then a police wagon screeched to a stop outside the bar with its siren blaring away.  'Doo Daa, Doo Daa, Doo Daa, Doo Daa'.
"What the..." said Alfred but before he could say anymore half a dozen police men tumbled into the bar carrying their musical instruments. They lined up around Alfred and blasted out '*For he's a jolly good fellow*'.

All the bar regulars stood up and sang along with the police musicians and applauded their much respected constable. Alfred was at first shocked and then embarrassed and then delighted that he had not been forgotten.
"Whose idea was this?" he asked.
"Everyone's" answered the Inspector "You've done a first class job of looking after this village over the years. We all want to say thank you."

And that is what they did. Each and everyone went over to shake his hand. The drinks were lining up. The band played *'Wish me luck as you wave me goodbye'* followed by a feisty rendition of the San Andrija Anthem. The musicians all shook Alfred's hand and wished him well as they piled back into the wagon and off they went.
"Come and sit here" called George pulling up a chair to the central table "Tell us what you are going to do now you are retired. You have all the time in the world now."
"Well I am not sure" said Alfred 'I need to get my breath back first."

"No. Not so" said Do "First you must eat something. My son Don has prepared a special buffet for you. Din open the curtains."

Din pulled back the curtains in front of the stage to reveal a magnificent spread of the most delicious food. It was so well presented that the bar broke out into spontaneous applause. "Wow!" exclaimed Harry "So all that studying has really paid off. Well done Don." Don smiled his father's happy smile.

As the patrons tucked into the food and supped more drinks, the conversation became even more lively and animated. "How long were you in the force then Alfred?" asked George. "Twenty five years or thereabouts" he replied "Joined in eighty nine but I had served ten years in the army before that. Loved every minute of it. Good times and bad." "I bet you saw a few New Years in then" said Aris. "You're right there, Aris" continued the constable "In the early years I patrolled Strait Street. But I guess none of you know where that is. Am I right Harry? George?" he asked with a twinkle in his eye. They laughed "Don't know what you are talking about constable. Not guilty." "Mmm, you can't fool me, gentlemen" he continued "No, some of the best times we had were with the sailors down the 'gut'. They were there to enjoy themselves and sometimes they got a bit rowdy but mostly they were just having a jolly good time." "Drink up Alfred" said Harry "You're a civilian now. You can get well and truly inebriated."

"Harry you are incorrigible" said Alfred "I will be careful though because I've seen what too much drink can do, remember. Some people get violent but most just get silly. And few remember what they did the next day."

He took a long sip of his Blue label.

"I recall one time when this army chap had had so much to drink that he could not stand. His pals sat him down in the gutter to try to sober him up and as they did so he started to recite a poem."

"Really!" said Aris "What was the poem?"

"Funny you should ask as I can remember every word. If I can remember rightly it went...

*One evening in October*
*When I was about one-third sober*
*And was taking home a load with manly pride*
*My poor feet began to stutter, so I lay down in the gutter*
*And a pig came up and lay down by my side*

*Then we sang "It's All Fair Weather*
*When Good Fellows Get Together"*
*Till a lady passing by was heard to say*
*'You can tell a man who boozes, by the company he chooses'*
*And the pig got up and slowly walked away.*

I think he came from Cornwall but he was clear as a bell. Then he passed out. Apparently the next day he had no recollection of saying the poem and denied that had ever heard it. That's what drink can do."

"When I've had too much I just want to sing" said Pawlu.

"Don't let him sing" interrupted Carmena "He will clear the bar if he does."

"Well there's no music anyway" said George "Hey Ho, where's the music."

Ho shrugged his shoulders and grimaced. With Tonio and his band absent Ho had forgotten to provide any musical entertainment.

"You used to play piano George" said Harry "Give is a tune."

"Not any more" said George. "Not since Arthur got me."

"Arthur! Who's Arthur?" said Aris.

"Arthur. You know Arthur –  Arthur– Itis" smiled George.

"I can play if you want" No lights who had been quietly sitting in his corner seat stood up.

"I didn't know you could play piano, No Lights" said Pawlu "You have kept that quiet."

"I have not had cause to mention it before" he replied "I often play at home to keep myself amused. I only know old songs though."

"That's OK with us" said George "We are all old as well."

A couple of months earlier when Do had been cleaning behind the stage she had discovered an old upright piano buried under a pile of moth eaten curtains. It was covered in dust but all the notes seemed to be working. Ho was delighted with the find and called in a tuner to revive it. He also had it painted in a bright yellow gloss paint.

"Yerrow ve'y rucky for Chinaman" beamed Ho.

Aris was also delighted.

"It will match my purple Bass" he observed.

   Harry took No lights by the arm and led him to the piano stool where he adjusted himself and began to play. As No Lights struck the first chords he said

"This one is for you Constable Alfred."  He could not have picked a better tune to start with. It was from the musical 'Oliver',

'*Consider yourself at home. Consider yourself one of the family'.*

   The entire bar joined in, raising their glasses to Alfred who reciprocated by raising his glass and calling for drinks all round. No Lights continued playing, the patrons continued singing, Ho continued pouring drinks as the midnight hour approached.

"Great night Harry" said George who was by now well lubricated

"By the way where are Angus and Joan. It's New Year they should be here."

"They are on their way" said Harry above the noise "Had something to do at the kennels."

And as if on cue, Angus and Joan entered the bar.

"Over here" Harry called "thought you were going to miss it."

"Och, no. I wouldny miss celebrrating Hogmanay with my best friends now would we Joan."

"Absolutely not" said Joan giving her brother a big hug.

"Is Bung OK" asked Harry.

"Aye. He has a few beers and a very big sausage as a treat for Farrt" replied Angus "And strict orders to keep Farrt well away from the dogs."

   No lights was enjoying his new fame as a bar pianist. Ho looked at his watch and rang the bar bell for attention.

"Twenty seconds to go, my flends. Get leddy."

"Ten, nine , eight, seven....."

The entire bar joined in.

"Three , two, one....Happy New Year."

A crescendo of 'Happy New Years' *'Is-Sena It-Tajba'.* raised the roof. The church bells rang out to welcome in the New Year. The patrons spilled out into the *pjazza.* No Lights played *Auld Lang Syne.* All the worries of the world were forgotten as the villagers of Ħal -Luqa submerged themselves into a wonderful warm marshmallow cushion of happiness and joyful revelry.

"Hey everybody" shouted Mario "This is the Ho Chi Do Chi Bar let's do the Hokey Cokey. Play it, No Lights."

As Mario led the revellers round the bar tables out into the street, across the pjazza and down Triq San Gużepp, it was inevitable that they would wake up old Guisseppa. As the unofficial representative of the Triq San Gużepp neighbourhood watch, known also as 'nose ache', it was her duty to see what was going on. She carefully opened her shutters to see what all the noise was about. But on this occasion she smiled as she saw all the villagers of Ħal-Luqa enjoying themselves. Nothing to worry about. After all it was the New Year. No need for any Hail Mary's. The rosary beads could remain under the pillow.

She closed the shutters and returned to the comfort of her bed. The revellers revelled until the early hours. Another year had started– just like last year and the year before and the year before that. In Malta traditions are conscientiously maintained – especially if they involved food and drink!

# The Case is Closed

The walk from Santa Lucia to Ħal-Luqa takes about thirty minutes if you go at a leisurely pace. It was a journey that was regularly taken by John Spiteri who used to be the village constable at Ħal-Luqa. The reason for his journey was his obsession with catching the Barber/Nora gang who had plagued his life when he was in office. In spite of his being retired from the force and having spent time in the Mount Carmel home for the disturbed, he still could not give up his mission to bring Harry and Nora to justice.

No-one knew why he had it in for Harry nor Nora for that matter. They were both law abiding citizens although maybe Nora did drive rather erratically and both she and Harry parked on yellow lines- apart from that they were fine examples of good citizenship. Nevertheless Spiteri had perceived with his obsession. To the villagers he had become a harmless figure of fun with his constant surveillance of the village, looking for any sign of a misdemeanour by Harry, notebook and pencil always at the ready. His antics had brought many a smile to the villagers as they observed him dodging from doorway to doorway, hiding behind statues, pretending not to be there. But Spiteri knew that one day, oh yes! one day Harry Barber would slip up. And he would be there to record and report it.

So it was that the constable had set up his observation position opposite the police station where he had good view of the Ho Chi Do Chi Bar- the headquarters of Harry's gang. He had hidden in the red telephone box outside the side entrance to the church where he knew he was safe as nobody used it nowadays, everyone had a mobile! The currant red Telephone box had been a fixture in the village since before the war. For many it had been the only source of communication. Indeed villagers would queue to use it at one time and while they waited for their turn they would tuck into their cheesecake or pizza's and chat with their neighbours, catching up on the latest gossip or solving the world's problems. That handset could tell a treasure trove of personal stories. The red telephone box together with the red pillar box, both symbols of the British presence were an essential part of village life. Taken for granted today no doubt but it would take a brave man to remove them.

The constable had settled into his hideaway, patiently waiting for anything that might put him on the trail of Harry Barber. But as the morning drew on and nothing happened he decided to take a break and popped out of his hiding place for some pastizzi.

"Ah! Constable Spiteri" said Zeppi the owner of the pizza parlour "Good to see you. Haven't seen you around here for along time" he lied knowing full well of the constable's activities.

"Thank you Zeppi. But I must ask you to keep a low voice. I am on an undercover assignment" advised the constable "Please you have not seen me. I will have four pastizzi, jekk jorġgħbok."

As he went to take out his wallet to pay for his cheese cakes he realised he no longer had it. It must have fallen out of his back pocket.

" My wallet has gone" said Spiteri "Please hold the pastizzi for me. I will have to go and see if I can find it."

"OK no problem" smiled Zeppi.

The constable ran across to the telephone box but there was no wallet. Spiteri was puzzled. Where could he have  lost it? Maybe on the walk to the village. He would have to retrace his steps. But first he would do what any sensible person would do and that was to go to the police station to see if it had been handed in. After all the people of Ħal-Luqa were good honest people, with exception of Harry  Barber of course, so if they had found it they would have handed it in to the station.

Constable Ellul had just  poured himself his morning cup of coffee when John Spiteri entered. Constable Alfred  pretended not to recognise him as he knew of his antics and enjoyed playing along with his game.

"Good Morning sir" he said "What can I do for you?"

Spiteri glanced around to see if anyone was listening and satisfied that they were alone said "It is me, Constable Spiteri. You remember I was the village constable before you took over."

" I remember the name" said Alfred looking puzzled "But I do not recognise the face. Have you any indentification?"

" Well no. I don't" answered Spiteri "My ID is in my wallet which I have lost so that is why I am here to see if anyone has handed it in."

"Mmm. Difficult. You see without ID I cannot verify your identity and I certainly can't hand over any property until you can confirm it" Alfred was loving it.

"But surely you know me. I was the one who nearly caught the Barber/Nora gang, but they conspired to have me locked up" pleaded Spiteri "Surely you remember."

"Well, I do have a wallet that was handed in this morning" said Alfred knowing full well that this was Spiteri's wallet. "Let's have a look inside. Now what is this?" he said taking out an ID card.

"Yes, that's  me" said Spiteri looking over Alfred shoulder.

"I am not so sure" mumbled Alfred stroking his chin "This person is a lot younger. He has hair for one thing. You are nearly bald and you have a big walrus moustache."

"That is because I am in disguise" explained Spiteri getting rather agitated.

"In disguise! Why are you in disguise?" asked Alfred "Are you mafiosa?" Constable Ellul pulled out his truncheon " Are you an escaped criminal? You are on the run aren't you?" He reached for the telephone "I think I will need back up. It looks like I have a dangerous criminal on my hands" Alfred was milking it for all his worth. He pretended to dial a number.

"Hello, Is that Floriana Police headquarters? I need urgent assistance. I have an escaped maf osa god father in my station and I need back up to control him. Send some men this is very urgent."

Spiteri was going crazy. Why was it that everyone misunderstood him? Why did everyone think he was bonkers?

"No please, Constable. Stop" pleaded the desperate man " It is me, John Spiteri. Surely you remember" he cried in exasperation "I will go and get Zeppi from the Pizza Parlour he will vouch for me" The ex constable made for the door.

"Stop where you are" shouted Constable Ellul "As far as I know you are a danger to the public. I cannot have criminals roaming the streets of Luqa. I have a duty to perform and I will have to put you under arrest."

Just then Harry Barber passed by the station. Spiteri spotted him and called out.

"Harry Barber, help" he shouted.

Harry was taken aback. Was that Spiteri? What was going on? He entered the police station where John Spiteri was standing with his back to the wall, clearly distressed and almost in tears.

"Harry Barber, you have to help me" he pleaded "The constable thinks I am a mafia agent and he wants to arrest me. I need someone to tell him who I am before the flying squad arrive." Alfred tipped a wink at Harry who was never slow on the uptake.

" Well" said Harry drawing a deep breath "This is a difficult situation that we have here. I need to think about it. I seem to remember a constable named Spiteri but he did not look like you as I recall."

"That's because I am in disguise" screamed a frustrated Spiteri.

"And why are you in disguise, may I ask?" said Harry.

"So you won't recognise me when I arrest  you" exploded Spiteri. No sooner had he said the words that he realised what he had said.

"Ah! Now I remember. You are the one who has been plagueing me and Nora all these years. Making our lives a misery and without any justification. That poor woman went to her grave with your accusations hovering over her" Harry was on a  winning streak "And now *you* want *me* to do you a favour!"

"Please Mr Harry, sir" Spiteri was on his knees "I am sorry. I was just doing my duty. I can't go back to Mount Carmel. You have to save me."

"Mmm. Well let's see if I can think of something that will jog my memory" mused Harry. " What if you promise to stop hounding me, withdraw all your insinuations and never again accuse me of anything."

" Yes, yes of course. Anything you say but please tell the constable to call off the back up."

"Right. But on one condition" said Harry "We will forget the past and you and I will go to Ho Chi's bar and have a drink together. What about it?"

"Thank you. Of course. I will never trouble you again and I will apologise to Nippy Nora next time I go to the cemetery" said a very relieved ex constable. He stood up and shook Harry's hand vigorously. To the constable's surprise it felt like a great burden had been lifted from his shoulders. This simple frontal encounter with Harry had left him feeling liberated– more than years of counselling at the mental home had achieved. For the first time in years he smiled and for that he could thank Harry Barber. The case was closed. No more subterfuge, no more disguises, no more creeping around the village.

Alfred picked up the telephone and said "Floriana Headquarters. This is Constable Afred Ellul, Ħal–Luqa Police station. Emergency over, peace and harmony have been restored. Please call off the back up" He winked at Harry.

"Here is you wallet Mr Spiteri" said the constable "I suggest you pick up your pastizzi and enjoy your drink with Mr Barber. You are a very lucky man. If Mr Barber had not been here to verify your ID you could well  have been locked up in Corradino prison for a great many years.

And so it was that Harry and the ex constable had their drink at Ho's bar like two old pals much to the amazement and amusement of the villagers.

# Harry goes to the Dogs

"I just don't know where the time goes" complained George.

"It goes by" answered Aris "Says so in the song."

"Thank you Einstein" said George "Very helpful. No, I mean once I retired I thought I would have all the time in the world to relax and do nothing yet every day seems to get busier and busier."

"I know exactly what you mean, George" added Harry "Since I inherited all that money and set up the kennels I have not had a minute to myself. Sometimes I wish I hadn't started."

"But it was your dream, you said" taunted Aris.

"Some dream" answered Harry "It's turned into a nightmare if you ask me."

"Oh come on, come on" said Idaho "You don't mean it. It has been great. You have your kennels, some of the finest greyhounds I've ever seen and most of all you met your sister and her family after all these years. What are you complaining about, mate?"

"Well, yes you are right" agreed Harry "Mustn't complain really. I guess it is February and everything looks grey this time of the year."

"Exactly" encouraged Aris "But, spring is just round the corner. Everything to look forward to."

"Aye" added Angus "And we can start trrraining the dogs now. They are a year old so they are rrready. Before you know it we will be rrracing them at the new rrrace trrack."

"That's what I mean" said George "A year old and yet it only seems like yesterday that they were born."

"Well, here's a man who knows all about being busy" Andrew, the Mayor entered the bar.

"Gentlemen" he greeted "How are we all? Full of the joys of spring I trust."

Harry was always impressed with the irrepressible enthusiasm of the Mayor. Nothing seemed to faze him. Whatever the problem he had a solution. It was his positive outlook on life that had inspired Harry to go all out for the greyhound stadium and all that it involved. His trust in the Mayor was not misplaced.

"Why these melancholy faces?" observed the ample Marella who had followed her husband into the bar.  "Cheer up Harry. Tell your Aunty Marella all about it."

Harry shuddered.

"Oh! Take no notice of me, Marella" said Harry "Just feeling a bit sorry for myself."

"Then you must let me cheer you up" offered Marella pulling up a chair close to Harry. "Now, what is it that is keeping you down in the dumps?"

"He is beginning to wonder if his idea for the kennels was the right one" explained Aris.

"Yes, you see a year ago he had a choice of finding a bride or opening a kennels" added George "In his wisdom he chose to go to the dogs."

"You silly man" laughed Marella "You can have the best of both worlds. The dogs and a wife. Marella wi l find a nice Maltese lady for you. You will be very happy. You'll see."

Harry's despondency was reaching new depths as he contemplated the thought. George was loving it.

"There's your chance Harry" said George mischievously "You should take her up on her offer. Think about it. Someone to cook for you, someone to clean up after you, someone to keep you warm in winter. Who knows it could very well be the making of you."

"No thanks" said Harry clearly embarrassed "I appreciate the offer Marella but I am too old and set in my ways now."

"Then you must come to me when you need someone to talk to" added the very naughty Marella giving Harry a knowing wink. The Mayor joined the table with a tray of drinks for everyone.

"Harry" he said "I am glad I bumped into you. I have some news. The stadium is nearly finished. They are putting in all the finishing touches now and I want to take you, Joan and anyone else for that matter for a conducted tour next week. When can you come?"

"Whenever it suits you Andrew" said Harry relieved to change the subject.

"Then let's say Tuesday. We can leave at about ten. Is that too early?" said Andrew.

"No, that is fine" replied Harry "I look forward to it."

Suddenly Harry felt a lot better. The Mayor had cheered him up, he had thwarted Marella's plans for his future and fended off George's mischievous meddling.

"Have ye any idea when the stadium will open, Mr Mayor?" asked Angus.

"We are hoping to have the first race day in August" answered the Mayor "In fact we are trying to make it on the fifteenth which is the feast of Santa Marija."

"That would be fantastic" said Harry "That is the day that the SS Ohio sailed into Grand Harbour with supplies to relieve the suffering of the Maltese during the war."

"So what has the Ohio coming into Grand Harbour got to do with a greyhound stadium?" asked a puzzled George .

"Well, nothing directly but it only managed to stay afloat with the help of other ships that were lashed to it. Just like my idea would never have survived if it hadn't been for all my friends and supporters" said Harry raising his glass to everyone in the bar. A great cheer went up as everyone responded.
"And let's not forget Bungalow and Fart" he added.
"How could anyone forget Fart!" said George.
Another cheer went up for Bungalow and his faithful but rather smelly mongrel.

Tuesday could not come soon enough. Harry had arranged to take Joan, Angus, George and Idaho in his Chevrolet. Aris loaded Bungalow, Fart, Pawlu and Carmena in his Morris and Loretta brought Ho, Do and the twins in her taxi. All well suited and booted they set off for the tour of the new stadium. Andrew and Marella had made their own way there.

As the Luqa convoy drove into the old airfield of Ta Qali they were rendered speechless at the sight of the new stadium. It was formidable.
"Wow!" gasped George "That is magnificent. What have you done here, Harry?"
"Blimey!" said an impressed Harry "Never imagined anything like this. It is huge."
"It makes Piano's entrance to Valletta look amateurish" added Aris, admiring the vast extent of the new structure.

The stadium really was a magnificent piece of architecture. Constructed of a mixture of glass and concrete, the flowing lines and curves of the building were not overbearing despite their size. The glass which was tinted to offset the heat of summer reflected the blue sky and surrounding areas in such a way that the enormity of the building was minimised. The entrances, of which there were several, were clearly marked and a large car park surrounded the building.

"I thought the Lufthansa building at Ħal-Farruġ was big but this, well, I think it is bigger" exclaimed Idaho.

"There's Andrew and Marella" said Harry "Come on we must join them."

"There are a lot of cars in car park, Harry" said Joan "I thought we were the only ones coming. Looks like there are more."

Andrew greeted the *Luqajin* and directed them to the main entrance.

"What do think Harry?" asked the Mayor "What are your first impressions? Pretty amazing, eh? Bigger than you ever imagined."

"I am speechless Andrew" said Harry "Whoever designed this deserves a medal. It is, well, it is amazing."

"Let's get inside for the reception" Andrew ushered them into the stadium "Then I will show you round."

"Reception! I didn't know it was reception" said Harry "I thought we were just here to take a look around."

"Well you are" said Andrew "But first we have a welcome committee with some drinks and food and then we do the tour. Didn't Don tell you?"

Harry turned to see Don standing behind him. He wore one of his father's widest smiles. Harry was intrigued.

"Sorry Mr Harry" said Don "I wanted it to be a surprise for you."

"Well it certainly is" answered Harry "What part did you play in all this?"

"You will see" said Don giving the sign of the Great Guisseppa. Carmena chuckled.

"Who are all these people Andrew?" asked Harry puzzled by the vast turnout.

"They are all people who have an interest in the project" said Andrew "I will introduce you to them later. But first you must come with me."

The Mayor led Harry and Joan over to a podium where there was a table and a microphone. He tapped the mic to check it was working and then addressing the assembled party said–

"Ladies and Gentlemen, may I have your attention for a moment please." Everyone turned to listen to what the Mayor had to say. "You have been invited here to see our magnificent new stadium and to meet some of the many people who have been involved in its construction. It has been a long journey but I know you will agree with me it has been worth it. I promise I will not talk too much."

"I'll drink to that" called George

"Thank you George. Mine's a Scotch" laughed Andrew "But there is a person who I want you all to meet. Harry Barber."

Andrew embraced Harry as he pulled him towards the mic. Harry was clearly embarrassed.

"Harry is the one who dreamt up the whole project and it is thanks to him that we now have one of the best greyhound stadiums in Europe."

A great cheer emitted from the assembled guests.

"Speech" they cried "Speech."

The Mayor directed Harry towards the mic. Reluctantly he picked it up and started to speak only to realise he had the mic upside down.

"Sorry" he said "Never used a mic before. Never spoke in public before either. Erm. Erm. Just want to say thank you for all your support especially to Joan my sister whose encouragement made me go ahead. And to all the *Luqajin.....*"

A great cheer rang out.

"Thanks guys for being such good friends."

  He handed the mic back to Andrew. Much as Harry was enjoying the attention and newly found fame he still had that niggling thought that his dogs may not be pedigree greyhounds and if so then his reputation would plummet if anyone found out. But for the moment it was better that he put the matter to the back of his mind.

Marella who was immaculately dressed in a pink trouser suit, took the mic and said-

"Please help yourselves to the buffet which has been prepared by our chief Chef, Don Chi" she pointed to Don who gave a polite bow "Let's have a cheer for Don." An appreciative cheer rang out for Don and his magnificent spread. "And the bar is open" shouted Marella above the noise, loving every minute of it. "Three cheers for Harry Barber and the Ta Qali Greyhound stadium."

Her ample voice matching her ample proportions.

She clasped Harry's wrist and pulled him towards her ample bosoms for an affectionate kiss and hug. Harry did not see it coming but managed to wrestle free as she came in for a second go. Harry deftly sidestepped the attempt and realising that was all she was going to get, the ample Marella threw her ample arms in the air as yet another cheer rang out. The guests made for the bar and the tables loaded with food.

Don had prepared a sumptuous feast. A truly magnificent variety of Maltese, English, Chinese, Italian and Spanish dishes. An international spread of the most delicious titbits.Bungalow noticed several versions of sausage rolls and surreptitiously slipped a few into his pockets. He would feed them to Fart later. He had the good thinking to leave Fart in the car just in case he caused trouble. Any emmissions from his rear end would not be appreciated. A wise move.

As the guests tucked into the feast, the room was alive with animated conversation. Harry noticed that apart from the Maltese people there were several other nationalities present, most noticeably Italian and German. Clearly Andrew had been hard at work publicising the venture.

"Who is that tall gentleman over there by the bar" asked Harry "The one with that rather magnificent  moustache?"

"You may well ask" laughed Andrew "He is your biggest rival. His name is Ludvig Schafer. He is from Hamburg and he has set up his own kennels in Gozo. Do you want to meet him? I think you should."

"Yes of course" said Harry beckoning George and Angus to come with him.

"Herr Schafer" said Andrew "*Entschuldigen Sie, bitte.* May I introduce you to Harry Barber who will be racing his dogs against yours."

"It is a pleasure to meet you, sir" replied Herr Schafer who stood to attention, bowed politely and shook Harry's hand vigorously "At last we meet."

Harry checked if any fingers had been broken and answered.

"Pleased to meet you too. This is my sister Joan and her husband Angus." Joan avoided the hand shake.

"I hear you are from Hamburg" said Angus.

"Ja. I was born there" Herr Schafer smiled and as he did so his moustache twitched a sort of dance under his nose."Have you been there?"

"Many times" said Angus "But I kept getting run over by bicycles."

The German laughed "Ah yes they have priority, of course."

"What brought you to Malta" asked Joan.

"I saw an article about the proposal for the greyhound stadium on the Internet" explained Herr Schafer "So I got in touch with Herr Andrew and decided it was an exciting venture. I brought six of my dogs and set up my kennels in Gozo where I have a holiday villa."

"So you have been to the islands before" said Angus.

"Ja. Many times. It is like a second home for me" his moustache was doing its dance again.

"Herr Schafer, it is good to meet you and I guess we will meet many times more" said Harry shaking his hand cautiously "We must go and have a look around now."

"*Schon Sie zu treffen, mein freund. Auf wiedersehen*" replied Herr Schafer. Harry expected him to click his heels but instead he did another jig with his moustache.

"What a nice man" said Joan obviously impressed with Herr Schafer's good manners.

"Mmm. I think he will prove a substantial adversary" said George "He obviously knows his stuff."

"As long as he does not look too closely at my dogs" said Harry apprehensively.

"Never mind that" said Angus "Let's have a look at what you have started here, Harry Barber."

If the exterior of the building was impressive then the interior was even more so. There was a massive entrance and reception hall which led into the viewing and catering area where punters were able to choose from five different restaurants. Two of them were under the management of Don and offered either a Maltese or a Chinese menu. The other three comprised of an English traditional fare, a Spanish selection or an Italian menu. The dining tables were arranged in a circular layout enabling every diner to view the race track. Punters could order their meals and bet on line from their tables without leaving their seats. It was state of the art technology. For those who were less conversant with computers a team of waiters and attendants were at hand to take orders and place their bets.

The circular race track was five hundred metres in length and could easily be seen from the viewing balconies. Punters could also view from around the track itself where the bookies set up their booths. Massive television screens were everywhere so no one would miss a thing.

Apart from the racing, the stadium had been designed to hold other events. The corporate entertaining prospects had been catered for as well as weddings, private functions and presentations. The promotional activity through the Internet and local and international communication had been placed firmly on Din's shoulders. A massive responsibility for one so young. But her qualifications that she had worked so hard for would hold her in good stead. She would also have the support of her parents Ho and Do who knew a thing or two.

"I tell you what, George, this is bigger than I ever imagined it would be" Harry was overwhelmed "Andrew has excelled himself. I really must congratulate him."

"Nice of you to say so, Harry" the Mayor joined them "Not all down to me. A very large team of very experienced experts have drawn this up. That's why it has taken so long. Wanted it to be right from the word go."

"And when will the word 'go' be" asked Angus.

"Glad you asked" said Andrew "It has been confirmed as we hoped, for the fifteenth of August. The feast of Santa Marija."

"Then we must get to work training the dogs Angus" said Idaho "No time to lose."

"But before we do let's have a one more drink to celebrate" said Harry.

"Yes, but which bar?" said George 'There seems to a different bar every time I turn around.This is heaven on earth."

"Come to my bar" called the ample Marella "I have chosen Don's bar as my own special bar. I'll have a G&T, heavy on the G light on the T. You know me, don't you Harry."

For once Harry was happy to oblige. He had a good feeling about this place. Maybe everything would be OK after all.

Having satisfied their appetites and drunk a few more bevies the *Luqajin* decided to make their way back to Luqa. Harry raised his glass to Herr Schafer who was at the far end of the room and who responded by raising his glass and giving a fine jig with his moustache.

Fart was asleep on the back seat of Aris's Morris estate. He lazily raised his head as Bungalow approached but then he caught whiff of the sausages in Bungalow's pocket. He was wide awake now, tail wagging in anticipation of a feast of his favourite food. Sausages.

Bungalow took the sausages from his pocket and gave them to a very grateful dog. Harry began to laugh.

"What are you laughing at, Harry?" asked Joan.

"Like minds think alike" said Harry pullirg two more sausage rolls from his pocket at which point Aris, George and Idaho did the same.

No one had forgotten Fart. In true spirit of the *Luqajin* a pile of sausages had been produced. In Luqa no one is forgotten. None the least Fart the dog.

# The Waiting Game

The thermometer that hung on the wall of the Ho Chi Do Chi Bar was nudging forty two degrees Centigrade. It was to be expected of course. The celebrations of Saint Andrew's feast were the signal for the sun to turn up the heat.

  By mid July the island would become a furnace from which any escape was virtually impossible. Every breath of air was hot and dry. Throats were dry, eyes were dry, perspiration dried up immediately. The heat rose from the pavement and scorched the skin. Everyone carried water with them. Everyone walked in the shade. Everyone had a plan to keep cool. The well proven method of closing shutters and windows to keep the house interior dark and cool was well known to every Maltese house wife. Some made for the coast for a dip into the ever welcoming and cooling waters. Air conditioning helped of course but it was expensive. Better to go to a supermarket or best of all, the cinema, where the air con gave some respite from the oppressing heat. It mattered not what film was being shown. An armful of pop corn, nuts and Kinnie would be enough to while away a couple of hours in the cool. What better way to spend your siesta!

Harry was acclimatised to the heat and it really did not trouble him at all. For George it was a different matter and he cursed the months of July and August. He was always looking for ways to keep cool. His trouble was that he tended to look at his pint of beer taken from the refrigerator and placed carefully in front of him. He would stare in envy at its coolness.

"I think I have got it" said George.

"Well, keep away from me" said Harry" I don't want to catch it."

"No, no. It's the heat" explained George "I think I have an answer."

"Go on, Einstein" urged Harry "What is it?"

"You get yourself a large plastic bag and fill it with ice" explained George "Then you get a small hand pump with a spray nozzle on the end of a pump. Put it in a haversack and carry it on your back. Then as you walk along you can hold the spray over your head and as the ice melts you pump away and you get a cooling shower. Job done."

"So it doesn't matter that your shirt gets soaking wet!" said Aris. He wasn't referred to as Aristotle for nothing!

"Maybe but in this heat it will dry again in ten seconds" said George confident that he had found the solution to Malta's heat problems.

"Actually, you are closer to a solution than you think" added Pawlu "You see, Angus was worried about the effect of the heat on the dogs so I built a shower room for them. It sends a very fine spray of cold water which keeps them cool. Their kennels also have air conditioning. No expense spared."

"Sounds wonderful" said George "I think I will move in with the dogs."

"Well done Pawlu. That is good thinking" added Harry "I am a bit worried that when race day does come it will be too hot for the dogs to race."

"No worries" said Pawlu "I mentioned this to Andrew and he said that the race track itself has a system that will spray cool water over the dogs as they race round the track. The track will dry up almost immediately. So it should be fine."

"He seems to have thought of everything has our Andrew" said George "No wonder he is Mayor of Luqa."

"Do you fancy a trip up to the kennels, lads?" asked Harry "Let's see how the dogs are doing and get an update from Angus and Idaho."

"Sounds good to me" said George downing the rest of his beer. "See you later Ho."

The lads all piled into Harry's Chevvy and off they set for the cliffs of Dingli.  The farm where Harry had built his kennels was at the edge of the Dingli cliffs which was one of the highest parts of the island. It had turned out to be a well chosen spot for the dogs as the air was cleaner, fresher and cooler here. As the Chevvy pulled into the yard the dogs ran excitedly to the compound fence to greet their visitors. Greyhounds may appear to be aloof to many but they are amongst the most friendly and loyal of animals. Angus and Joe came out of the office to see what the fuss was about.

"Hi Angus" greeted Harry "Thought we would come and see how you are getting on."

"Fine. Couldn't be better" answered Angus wiping his forehead "Come into the office. It is cooler in there."

"The dogs are looking good" observed George "Your hard work is paying off by the looks of it."

"Aye. Thank you George" answered Angus "I think we have a winning team here."

   Indeed the dogs looked magnificent. They were nearly eighteen months old now and at the peak of their fitness. In spite of Harry's misgivings about their parentage, the likeness to Fart was not obvious. Much of this was due to Idaho Joe shaving the excess hair that the dogs had inherited from Fart and to the careful diet meticulously planned by Joe.

"They are a credit to you Angus and to you Joe" said Harry "Look at them. So proud. So regal. They look like those pictures you see of the ancient Egyptians. You know the ones where they are standing with the pharaohs at the royal palace looking so majestic"

"Aye, I believe greyhounds are descended from Egypt so maybe you are right" added Angus.

"Trouble is Fart is not Egyptian" remarked George "He is Maltese through and through."

At the mention of Fart's name Bungalow popped his head round the doorway.

"Hi Bung, old chap" greeted Harry 'Come and join us. We were just thanking Angus and Joe for all their hard work but we should thank you as well."

"No problem" said Bungalow blushing under his suntanned face "I just guard them and feed them once in a while. They seem to like sausages best of all."

Harry was about to explode.

"What" he said in disbelief "Please don't tell me you feed them sausages."

"Only once in a while" answered Bungalow puzzled by Harry's anger "It is their treat. They love them."

"I bet they do" chuckled George "Like father like son!"

"Did you know about this Angus?" asked Harry.

"Aye" answered Angus somewhat sheepishly "I only found out recently and Bung has stopped giving them now. Don't worry Harry. It will be OK. Look at them. Maybe a little plump round the middle but nothing to worry about. Only an expert would know that things were maybe not a hundred per cent. It will be alright on the night."

Harry was not so sure. What if the stewards found out! He would never live it down.

"I wish I had your conviction Angus" mused Harry "I need a drink to calm my nerves. Come on lads, time to get back to Ho and a cool beer."

"Can we pop in to Ta Qali on the way back for a last look at the stadium before the big day" said Aris.

"I guess so" said Harry "It is on the way. Ciao Angus, Joe, Bung. Remember Bung, no more sausages."

"OK Boss" replied Bungalow. Fart raised an ear at the sound of the word, sniffed the air, realised it was a false alarm and went back to sleep.

The short drive to the old airfield only took a few minutes and as they entered the stadium who should be arriving at the same time but Herr Schafer.

 "Good Morning, Herr Barber" greeted Herr Schafer. George chuckled to himself. Herr Barber, that's a good one. *Heqq,* if only he had some hair!

"Good morning to you, Herr Schafer" answered Harry ignoring George's smirking.

"No, please call me Ludvig" said the German politely.

"Thank you, Ludvig. I am Harry" continued Harry "I expect you are here for a final look before the big day."

"Ja. It is very exciting for both of us and for Malta" said Ludvig "You have achieved much. I am sure it will be a great success. Are you entering all the races by way?"

"No, just the first and last" replied Harry.

"So am I" smiled Ludvig, his moustache starting to dance. "What are the names of your entries?"

"One is called 'Thunder' and the other 'Lightning" said Harry.

"That is amazing" said Ludvig "My dog is 'Donner' which is German for 'Thunder' and the other is 'Blitzen' which means 'flash' like lightning. Such coincidence. I am beginning to like Malta more every day. Such good people. But one thing puzzles me."

"Oh what is that? Perhaps I can help" said Harry fearful that he had suspicions about Harry's dogs.

"It was at the reception. I could not help but notice that several people were putting sausage rolls in their pockets. Is it a Maltese custom? Should I have taken some?" asked Ludvig.

Harry began to laugh partly out of embarrassment that they had been seen taking the food and partly out of relief that his secret had not been exposed.

"It is a long story, Ludvig" he explained "You see Bungalow is our security guard and he has a dog named Fart."

"Fart!" said Ludvig "Why is Fart?"

"Well that's another story which you may well become aware of one day" continued Harry.

"I am thinking that 'Fart' in German  is 'Furz'" Ludvig was chuckling at the thought "You see a greyhound in German is 'wind hund'. So I am thinking that a 'wind hund' in Germany is a 'fart dog' ' in Malta. Most appropriate."

Ludvig laughed aloud at his quip. Harry joined in but could not help thinking how close Ludvig had come to the truth!

"Well, Fart and Bungalow are inseparable so where ever Bungalow goes, Fart, like the loyal dog that he is, is always at his side."

"Commendable" said Ludvig

"Ja. I mean yes" said Harry "Well we could not bring Fart in to the reception but we all know that Fart loves sausages. So we each smuggled some sausages in our pockets to give to Fart afterwards. You see he is one of the family. We could not leave him out."

"I understand. You are good people. You take care of each other." said Ludvig "I like that. But surely sausages are not good for the dog. They will make him fat. You don't want a fat Fart, do you?"

"You can say that again" laughed George.

"Of course not but you see he has been brought up on sausages and cauliflower" said Harry "I can't see him changing now."

"Cauliflower! *Vas ist das* 'cauliflower'?" asked Ludvig.

"It's a large white vegetable" explained Harry.

"But dogs do not usually eat vegetables" queried Ludvig his moustache starting to twitch.

"But he is from Siġġiewi" said Harry as if that explained everything. The moustache was now doing a fandango!

"Too much. I am confused. I ask no more" Ludvig waved his hand "I must get to my dogs now and we will meet again on race day. *Ich gebe dir Guten Tag.*"

He shook Harry and George by the hand and strode off.

"Wow!" said Harry massaging his crumpled fingers "That was a close one. I thought he was on to us."

"You're becoming a paranoiac, Herr Barber" said George sucking his fingers in an attempt to get the blood flowing again. "Apart from us few, no-one suspects anything. You're secret is safe with us. Just act normal and all will be fine." George was doing his best to reassure Harry.

"Let's go and see if we can find Don" suggested George "He is probably in his kitchen."

   Don had suggested to the organising committee that the bars should be named after the countries whose fare they represented. They agreed and now Don himself was put in charge of three bars – the Bar Malti, Bar Ingliz and the Bar Ciniz. The other two– Bar Taljan and Bar Spanjol were under the management of Giovanni Benedetti who had studied catering with Don in Milan. It was a good combination as both students had passed with flying colours and had formed a strong friendship. The diners at the stadium were in good hands.

"Hi Don" called Aris spotting the lad as he made his way towards the Bar Malti.

"Ah! Mr Aris" said Don "What a surprise.  Come and see the kitchens. They are nearly finished now."

   The lad was clearly proud of what he was about to show to his friends from Luqa. Indeed he had every right to be as the kitchens were immaculate and packed with all the latest state of the art kitchen apparatus.

"This is amazing" observed Harry picking up an apple corer "Never seen so many gadgets."

"Thank you Mr Harry" said Don "My mother and father have helped me choose what I need. Their advice has been invaluable. We must not let you down, sir."

"No fear of that" said Harry "Good advice from your mum and dad but one thing Don, you must promise me that you will not let your dad start karaoke nights."

Don laughed "My mother will kill him if he even thinks of it."

"The bar looks great Don" remarked George "And you even have some English beer on draft. I could easily become a regular here."

"You will be most welcome Mr George" smiled Don "Ah! There is Din. Hey Din, over here."

As soon as Din recognised the visitors she rushed over and gave Harry a big hug.

"Uncle Harry" she said "So lovely to see you. And George and Aris. Is this a special occasion or are you just checking out my brother?"

"No need to check anyone "said Harry "You are both doing a great job. Even got your own web site I believe."

"True and it is already getting results" said Din "I have many bookings for the opening day. It will be a big occasion for us.  I must go now for a meeting with our other sponsors but we meet soon."

  As Din made off Harry could not help but remark how both of the twins had grown up into such fine young people. Ho and Do must be very proud of them.

"Have you noticed something about the twins Harry" said Aris.

"Apart from how nice they are, no I haven't anything" said Harry wondering what Aris was getting at.

"Neither of them has a mobile 'phone" said Aris "Most unusual in these days. I was of the impression that babies were being born with mobiles already attached. Everywhere you go nowadays youngsters seem to have a mobile attached to their ears or they are sending texts to each other."

"You are right" said George "Hey, Don, why do you not have a mobile."

Don laughed "Oh, don't worry, I have one but I switch off when I am at work. I want to concentrate on my job. I want no interruptions. Most impolite."

"If only the rest of the youngsters were like you" lamented George You can't walk down a street nowadays without bumping into someone using a phone, completely oblivious to anyone else.I reckon they will all have arthritic thumbs by the time they are forty."

"Time to go, lads" said Harry "I can sense a George rant coming on. See you Don."

As they drove back to Luqa Harry felt a lot more relaxed. Everything seemed to be going to plan at last.

"So not long now Harry" said Aris "Another month and Thunder and Lightning will show us what they are made of."

"A whole month" remarked Harry "I don't think I can take the strain."

"It will pass by before you know it" reassured George "A few more beery nights at Ho's and it will be on us. Come to think of it we haven't had any parties at Ho's for a long time. It was Saint Andrew's feast last time and that was at the beginning of July. We should have a celebration of some sort to break the waiting."

"I'll drink to that" said Aris "What do you suggest?"

"I tell you what" said Harry "If my memory serves me right the eighth of August is Do's birthday. I remember that because Ho told me that eight is a very lucky number for Chinese people and he married Do because she was born on the eighth day of the eighth month nineteen seventy. So if you take the birth year and add up one plus nine plus seven it comes to seventeen. Add one plus seven you get eight. Magic. That makes her very lucky. Ho sure knew what he was doing."

"He was no fool, was he?" laughed George.

"What do you think? Shall I ask Ho to hold a party for her?" asked Harry.

"Brilliant idea" said George "Let's go straight to the bar and get things going."

As Harry pulled into the square the great bells of Saint Andrew's church belted out the midday chimes. The bar was empty apart from a surprise visit from the Mayor and the Mayoress who were enjoying a lunchtime drink and snack.

"Hi, Andrew" greeted Harry "Don't often see you at this time of day. How are you both?"

"Ah, you have caught us" laughed Andrew "We had some spare time so we thought we would spend it with Ho and Do and catch up on all the gossip."

"But Do is out shopping" said the ample Marella "So Ho is looking after us."

"As it happens that is good to hear" said Harry somewhat furtively "I mean about Do not being here."

"How so?" asked Andrew.

"Well I believe it is Do's birthday on the eighth" explained Harry
"Am I right Ho?"

"Yes" replied Ho "But she ve'y shy. Not rike fuss."

"Nonsense" said Marella "Every woman likes a fuss. She will love it
especially when she knows it is my birthday on that day as well.
We will celebrate together."

"Ah now! That is a coincidence. We can tell everyone it is your
birthday celebration but it will really be a joint one" exclaimed
Harry "Tell me Ho, did you once tell me that Do is very lucky
because of her birth dates adding up to eight?"

"Ah so" replied Ho "It true. Eight ve'y rucky number in China. Do
ve'y rucky. Her favo'ite colour is also yerrow which also
rucky.That why I paint the piano yerrow."

"And she is married to you Ho" laughed Marella "That makes her
extremely lucky."

"I no argue with that" Ho smiled one of his famous smiles.

"When were you born Marella?" asked George.

"You don't have to answer that Marella" said Harry trying to spare
Marella's blushes "George. You should know better, you don't ask
a lady her age."

Marella laughed "You are a gentleman Harry. My knight in shining
armour. But I have no problem with my age. I also was born on
the eighth of August but in nineteen seventy nine. Why do you
ask?"

"Come on George you're the mathematician. What do the
numbers add up to?" asked Harry.

"Let's see eighth day, eighth month, that's two out of three!"
George was surprised "And nineteen seventy nine is one plus nine
-plus seven plus nine is twenty six and two plus six is…"
"Eight" he called out in disbelief "Marella you are lucky just like
Do. This will be a great party I think."
"I must drink to that" said Marella "Ho drinks all round. Mine is a
G and T, heavy on…." she did not finish her sentence as the
combined voices in the bar said "…the G and light on the T."
The noise of laughter drew the attention of the Kappillan who
happened to be passing by. He looked into the bar cautiously.
"Father John come in. We are planning a surprise for Do on her
birthday maybe you can come and give her a blessing" said Aris
"She will like that. It is Marella's birthday too."
"It will be my pleasure. When will it be?"
"On the eighth. But Do knows nothing about it" said Aris.
"Count me in I will keep mum" said the priest placing his
forefinger alongside his nose, raising his eyebrows and sealing
his lips. Ho was shocked. Was the priest a member of Carmena's
Order of the Great Guisseppa? Did he know the secrets of
Carmena's black plastic handbag? Perhaps it would be better not
to know, nor to ask. After all Chinamen were supposed to be
inscrutable. Instead he smiled!
Nothing else to do now but plan for the party. Do would
unwittingly help of course but most of all it would take Harry's
mind off the race day.

# Do's Do

"But I have not finished preparing for Marella's party" protested Do carefully laying out some dishes filled with nuts and crisps on the tables of the bar.

"Never mind that" said Din "Daddy will take care of the rest. It is your birthday as well and I am taking you out to buy your present. I want no argument." She gave a nod and a wink to Ho, who was busy behind the bar.

"It OK" he said "I finish. You go now but be back by half seven when Malerra come for her birthday cereblation."

It was approaching four thirty and Din had arranged to go to Żebbuġ where they would attend Mass at the church of St Philip and afterwards go to Din's favourite dress shop in the village. She calculated that it would take about two hours.

Din had bought herself an old Toyota V tz which was in good condition in spite of the number of miles on the clock. But then cars seemed to last forever in Malta. Some of the quarry lorries still in daily use were well over sixty years old. Yet still they did their duty carrying heavy loads up steep hills.

Many of the old colourful buses that used to be the delight of locals and tourists still carried their appreciative passengers around the island. It was a sad day when the government decided to take these wonderful workhorses off the road. In the nineteen fifties you could identify your bus by its colour. The green ones were for Sliema, the  orange ones for Żurrieq, the red ones for Rabat and so on.

If you saw a bus coming you knew exactly where it was going. No need to run for it if it was the wrong colour. Such a good system. Nowadays the traveller had to squint his eyes in the bright sun to check the number on the bus! Sometimes progress is not progress at all!

It was not often that Do had the chance to spend some quality time with her daughter so forasmuch as she wanted to complete the preparations for the party she was also very pleased to be able to take some time out.

"Make sure you finish the table decorations Ho" she commanded "Put out the yellow flowers and napkins. Check the food in the oven and...."

"Mummy" called Din "Come on. Leave it to Daddy. He has done it before. He knows what he is doing."

Secretly Do knew that Ho would do a good job. They had been married for nearly thirty years and had worked well together both in Hong Kong and in Malta. What could possibly go wrong? She decided to put it to the back of her mind and enjoy her expedition with her lovely daughter. She would also get to Mass. Something she had not done for a while. Working in the bar had meant she was always busy even though the church was only a dozen or so steps away. This would be a rare treat.

With Do safely out of the way in the capable hands of Din, Ho could now get on with decorating the bar. The trusty triumvirate of Harry, George and Aris arrived to lend a hand.

Balloons were inflated, streamers hung around the walls, a collage of pictures of Do from when she was a baby was placed over the bar. The ample Marella who was in on the deception had come to offer her services to the party planners. A gesture greatly appreciated by all except Harry who was nervous about her real intentions. He need not have worried as this was Do's night and Marella was intent on making it as enjoyable as possible.

Unkown to Ho or Do, Harry had obtained a photograph of the Chi family from when they lived in Hong Kong. He had copied, enlarged and framed it. He showed it to Ho who was delighted with it.

"Where shall I hang it, Ho?" asked Harry who had his hammer and nails at the ready "Over the bar or on the long wall?"

"On the rong wall, I think it rook better" answered Ho.

"How high Ho?" said Harry.

"Ah Yes" answered Ho, smiling.

"No, I mean how high Ho?" Harry repeated his question.

"Yes. That is him" smiled Ho "How you know him?"

"Who?" asked Harry puzzled.

"Not who.How Hi" answered Ho.

"Yes, how high? That's what I want to know" an exasperated Harry "Is it high or low?"

"Yes, It is Hi and Lo" said Ho "I think you meet them when you came to Hong Kong many years ago."

"What are you talking about Ho?" cried Harry "I want to know how high you want me to put the picture. Not your family history."

"Solly Mr Hally" smiled Ho "I understand now. How Hi Ho Chi is my uncle and Lo Li Do Chi is my aunt. There they are in the picture. You remember them I think."

"I think we are at cross purposes Ho, my friend" laughed Harry "Of course I recognise them now. Just tell me, shall I hang the picture here or do you want it higher or lower?"

"It good where is" answered Ho.

"Then I will fix it here" said Harry not wishing to confuse matters further.

"Ah so" said Ho,

"My thoughts exactly" replied Harry sarcastically.

Time was getting on and Din and Do would soon be returning. The busy conspirators had made a good job of the decorations and now retired to get ready for Do's arrival. It was decided that 'D' hour would be seven o'clock and so it was that all of those in the know had taken the seats by the designated hour.

Andrew and Marella would sit closest to the entrance so that even as she arrived Do would not catch on as she would be expecting the celebration to be in honour of the ample Marella.

Tonio had assembled his band, everyone had filled their glasses, even Fart had abandoned his Villa in front of the bar to join in the throng– but secretly he hoped there may be the odd sausage roll tossed his way!

Fart had this remarkable ability to sense when something big was going on and since such events usually involved sausage rolls he knew he would have to be extra vigilant and ready to pounce when someone dropped a piece of sausage. It was an infallible instinct that he had developed over the years.

The Kappillan wisely chose a seat some distance away from Fart. He was well aware of the obnoxious emissions that occasionally issued from the rear of that creature. He was no fool.

"Good evening Father" greeted Alfred "May I join you?"

"Of course" smiled the priest "But is it my company you seek or distance from Fart?"

"You should have been a detective Father" laughed the ex constable "I confess to a dubious motive."

 "Here she comes" called Idaho who had been keeping a look out. Din's Toyota Vitz pulled up outside the bar and the unsuspecting Do entered.

Ho signalled to Tonio and the band struck up with *'Happy Birthday to you'.* Everyone joined in. Do stopped in her tracks. She was speechless. She never expected this! It was Marella's birthday celebration, not hers. What was happening!

Marella rushed forward and gave Do a great big hug.

"Happy Birthday Do" she said "This is your surprise. All your friends are here.We can share our birthdays together."

Do blushed. As a naturally shy person she was at first rather embarrassed but then when she got over the initial shock and she realised that she was among her friends she relaxed. She turned to Ho and demanded

"Husband. Where my drink?" She looked to the bar but there was no Ho "Hey, where my husband?"

As she spoke Ho appeared resplendent in his Elvis Presley suit with the difference that is was bright yellow! Yellow shirt, yellow trousers, yellow shoes. Even his mock guitar was yellow. He strode over to No Lights' yellow piano and at a stroke of his right arm signalled to the band to strike up with Do's favourite Elvis song '*The Wonder of You*'.

Do was in tears. Whether it was from emotion or from the dreadful off tune singing of her husband was anyone's guess. It mattered not as everyone enjoyed this wonderful tribute from a man to his wife.

As Ho reached the crescendo Do rushed over to her husband and gave him a great kiss and hug. A rare moment of affection that was appreciated by all.

"More, More" shouted Idaho "Encore. Give us another one Ho. More rock and roll mate."

Ho was in his element. Nothing he loved more than singing songs of his idol. Do was not so keen but... well it was her birthday and she knew Ho meant well so why not.

"What you wan me sing" asked Ho looking at Do.

"Long ago and far away" suggested George who was quickly stifled by Harry.

"I like *'Blue Moon'"* said Do.

"You rike *Broo Moon* you have *Broo Moon*" replied Ho signalling to Tonio to start playing.

And so the mood of the evening was set. The Tony Marozzi All Star band continued to play a mixture of Trad Jazz and sing-along favourites as the villagers indulged themselves in fine drink and food that Ho had provided.

"Marella" called Do "It is your birthday too. You should choose a song."

"That is kind of you Do" answered the ample Marella "I think I would like one we can all join in."

"Oh no!" said George "She is going to choose *'The Stripper'*."

Harry went white as he gripped his beer in trepidation. He remembered the last time!

"My favourite tune is *'Chanson D'Amour'* and what is more I will sing it but you all have to join in with the *'rat tat tat ta taa'* part."

The ample Marella took the mic and began singing and to everyone's amazement she was very good. The patrons obediently joined in with the chorus and with the saxophone and clarinet accompaniment it sounded very good. Sandra who had left her baby in the capable hands of her mother-in-law joined her on stage for the last verse.

Carmen was delighted when Sandra placed the baby Louis Andrew into his nanna's arms. She was so proud of her grand son and treasured every minute she spent with him. He was so much like his dad, her son Tonio. This boy would be loved by so many. Not that he showed any sign of appreciation! In fact it always amazed Carmen that  a baby could sleep through the loudest of noises and yet be awakened in a silent room by the drop of a needle!

Such was the case this evening. The band, the singing, the noisy chatter, the clinking of glasses, the raucous laughter. Nothing perturbed the boy. He slept through it all. In fact he and Fart had much in common. Both had a single minded outlook on life – sleep and food! Sausages in the case of Fart and milk  for Louis. And why not? After all Fart had lived most of his life and Louis was about to live his. What better aspiration could he have than to eat and sleep! As the gentle melody of Marella's *Chanson D'Amour* interrurpted only by the ghastly bar chorus of *rat tat tat ta taa,* so Louis Andrew slept on in Carmen's arms in his own private world of baby adventures.

As Marella and Sandra finished a great cheer once again nearly raised the roof.

"That was my wife singing" said an astonished Andrew. He had no idea that Marella was such a good singer "Where did you learn to sing like that?" he asked.

"*Heqq*!" exclaimed Marella "See what I mean. All these years married and you have never heard me sing! I sing when I am cooking, when I am cleaning, when I am in my bubble bath. You are too wrapped up with your schemes and campaigns to take notice of your very talented wife."

"I guess that is me in the dog house" laughed Andrew bowing with respect to his wife "Move over Fart I am in trouble again!"

Fart took no notice. He had already seen the pile of sausage rolls on the table with the other food and delicacies. He needed to concentrate in case someone dropped one on the floor. He was coiled ready to pounce at a moment's notice. Years of practice had made him an expert.

Tonio's band had been playing for over two hours and it was time for a break. It was also the signal for Carmena and Pawlu to disappear into the kitchen where they collected two large birthday cakes one for each of the birthday girls. The cakes were impressive having been baked by Carmena herself but it was the decoration that was special.

The one for Marella was a replica of the island of Malta and was covered with red and white icing to represent the flag of Malta. She had even included the George Cross emblem in the top left corner. Do's cake was designed like the exterior of the Ho Chi Do Chi Bar complete with Fart's *Villa*. It was coloured in yellow icing which was Do's favourite colour and as Ho regularly pointed out was considered to be lucky.

As Carmena and Pawlu carried the cakes aloft into the bar, Tonio struck up the band with '*Happy Birthday*'. Everyone joined in ending with a great cheer and applause.

Do hugged the ample Marella, not easy as Do was diminutive alongside the Mayoress.

"Thank you all so much" Do said "Such a surprise. Did you know anything about this Marella?""

"Well I did hear a little whisper" she laughed giving the secret sign of the Great Guisseppa.

"Cut the cake. Cut the cake" chanted George.

"It is too good to cut" said Do "I think I will keep it forever."

"No chance" said Ho appearing with his samurai sword "Here Do, use my sword."

She was honoured. Not everyone got to handle Ho's precious sword. Do took the weapon and with a mighty sweep cut the cake in two.

"Can I have a go?" asked Marella taking the sword from Do. She did so with some apprehension as she recalled the last time she had seen Ho's ceremonial sword.

On that day it was Harry's sausage that was cut in two! She shuddered at the memory but putting aside her misgivings she took hold of the magnificent weapon. She too sliced her cake in half. The entire bar erupted in a great cheer. All except Fart of course who could not see any pleasure in eating sponge cakes. Where were the sausages?

He need not have worried. Din and Don proceeded to bring out a fine array of finger food to add to what had already been consumed. No-one would go hungry tonight. Inevitably there were sausage rolls and as every villager knew of Fart's desires, he was amply rewarded for his patience. Angus scooped up an assortment of food to take to Bungalow who was on guard at the kennels. It was just a matter of days now before the inauguration of Malta's Greyhound Stadium.

Bungalow had decided to leave Fart with Aris while he stood guard at Dingli. He knew Harry was worried about Fart getting in with the dogs again.

The ample Marella tapped her glass to get the attention of everyone. What with the band and the crescendo of voices it was not surprising that no-one heard her. She signalled to Ho who struck the bar bell. All eyes fell on Marella.

"My dear friends" she said, she also knew how to milk a crowd "I am sure Do will join me in thanking you for a wonderful evening. You have made our birthdays perfect. We love you all."

"Oh yes! I agree" added a blushing Do "We are two very happy people."

"And soon we can celebrate all over again when Harry's dogs Thunder and Lightning show us what they can do."

Yet another cheer rang out.

"Good old Harry"

"Best of luck old chap"

"Thanks everyone" said Harry "Mustn't forget my sister and Angus and of course Bungalow and well... everyone really."

"Here's to Bungalow and Fart. Don't forget Fart. He played his part too" said Pawlu.

More than anyone knows mused Harry suddenly becoming quite sober at the thought. But this was not the time for misgivings. What was done was done. Best to put on a brave face and accept whatever fate had in store.

"Come on Harry, Sandra wants you to choose the last song before we all drink up and go home" called Tonio.

"I think *Que Sera, Sera* is about right" answered Harry.

"I'll drink to that" said george.

George and Angus knew exactly what Harry was thinking and raised their glasses in approval.

# Race Day.

   Today was the big day. Harry was a bag of nerves. This was the day that he had planned for so many years. It was his dream about to come true.

"Cheer up Harry" said Idaho "It will be fine you'll see."

   Harry was not so sure. It could all go wrong especially if the stewards found out that his dogs were not pure bred greyhounds. Too late now though. He had to go through with it. There were plenty of helpers from the village so that was a comfort. He was grateful for the positive encouragement from Idaho Joe but then Joe was always the optimist.

   Aris and Bungalow had gone to the Dingli kennels to pick up the dogs while Harry, Idaho Joe and George headed for the stadium. Pawlu and Angus would join them later.

"Cheer up Harry" said George "We are going to have a great day. No one will notice anything amiss".

"Are you sure about that?" replied Harry "I am worried someone will notice they are not normal greyhounds. They may have the heads of a greyhound but their bodies are distinctly Fartish."

"You should have named them 'sons of Fart' I reckon. Might have got away with it then" said Idaho.

"You're a great help Joe" said Harry getting even more agitated.

"Oh! Come on Harry. Nothing to worry about, mate. Where does it say in the rule book that the dog has to be a pure bred greyhound? And anyway who is going to challenge it?" said Idaho "They will have to deal with me if they do."

"Thanks Idaho that makes me feel a lot better" replied Harry sarcastically.

"All we have to do is keep the dog blanket over the dogs until the off" advised Angus "That way no one will know."

Harry's sister, Joan, had made two blankets for the dogs to keep them warm in the winter. They were made out of the Campbell Tartan and edged with gold braid. Magnificent jackets for what they hoped would be magnificent dogs. They were just what were needed to divert attention away from the rather portly dimensions of the dogs. Idaho had done a good job shaving off the excess hair that they had inherited from Fart and as long as no-one looked too closely the dogs would pass for greyhounds. "Let's hope it works" said George with little conviction.

As Harry turned the Chevvy into the stadium grounds he noticed that the day's events had drawn a large crowd. The Maltese loved their sports – as long as they did not have to make any effort themselves. But more importantly they liked a flutter with the bookies. Gambling was now a major occupation in Malta and had brought much overseas interest into the islands economy. Greyhound racing was an ideal venue for such matters.

Having parked up the Chevvy, the conspirators made their way to the owner's enclosure to await the arrival of Aris, Bungalow and the dogs.

One of the pleasures of any race meeting is the vibrant atmosphere that prevails. The air of expectant excitement as the races are called. Punters conscientiously analysing the form of the dogs and constantly checking the bookies odds. Dog owners proudly mingling and net working and generally making sure everyone knew they were there. The ladies parading in their latest fine outfits and picking up the hot gossip from each other. And then there was Harry and his entourage, not really sure how they should behave and feeling rather out of place.

"Harry" a voice boomed out from the back of the crowd. "Hey! Over here my friend" It was Andrew, the Mayor of Ħal–Luqa.

"Andrew" greeted Harry "Boy am I glad to see you. I have never felt so out of place in my life. Who are all these people?"

"Don't be silly Harry" Andrew reassured him "You are as entitled to be here as anyone. If it wasn't for you none of this would have happened. Come on have a drink. And you Angus and George. I don't think I have met this gentleman. Seen you around but never introduced" Andrew extended a hand towards Idaho Joe.

"Idaho Joe, Mister Mayor" said Idaho "I've heard a lot about you though and I believe you also contributed to making all this happen. Well done mate. I'm an old pal of Harry and George. Originally from America and then from Oz."

"Very pleased to meet you, Idaho. Any friend of Harry is a friend of mine" Andrew shook his hand warmly.

As if Harry didn't have worries enough, he was now about to have them augmented by the ample Marella, Andrew's buxom wife. "Where have you been Harry? I have missed you" the ample Marella, beautiful and ample as ever closed in on Harry.

"Sorry Marella. I have been very busy what with the stadium and the kennels and preparing for today" explained Harry.

"Oh I am sure today will be a great success for you" she said "And afterwards we must get together for drinkies and really celebrate".

"That will be nice" said Harry, his voice almost a whisper as he determined to make for the exit as soon as the races were over in order to avoid the ample Marella's advances.

"You have entered for two races I believe Harry?" said Andrew.

"Yes, the first race and the last race. Thunder is running first and Lightning last" explained Harry.

"Such wonderful names" said Marella. "They must surely win with such names. I will have little flutter I think."

"So will I" said Andrew "Must support the home team eh! What do you say, Harry?"

"Of course" replied Harry. The pressure was mounting. Harry was beginning to wish he had never started it. Maybe if there was an earthquake or something he could just disappear. What if he was found out! What if there was a steward's inquiry! What if they

discovered the dogs were not pure bred greyhounds! What if......
No, it did not bear thinking about. The disgrace. He would have
let down the mayor who had leaned on all his contacts and pulled
every string he could to get the project to this stage. Only one
thing to do and that was to withdraw. Better to be accused of
backing out than of cheating. Harry set off to find the stewards
and put in his formal resignation from the race when who should
appear but Herr Schafer.

"So we meet again, *mein freund*' he bellowed, twitching his
moustache "*Wie geht es ihnen*, Herr Barber? Looking forward to
the races, Ja?"

"Ja" said Harry "I mean yes. But please call me Harry."

"My apologies Harry. This is your big day. You are to be
congratulated on your exciting idea" he continued "I cannot wait
for the first race. My dog Donner is running."

"Thank you Ludvig" replied Harry "And I will be racing my dog
Thunder."

"Wunderbar" guffawed Ludvig "together we will create a storm."
He reached out to shake Harry's hand and after the bone
crunching grip had lessened, Ludvig strode off towards the
starting gate.

Harry was in a quandary! Everyone was so hyped up with
excitement and expectation. How could he as the main mover in
this enterprise withdraw his dogs! So many jobs depended on its
success. His name would be mud.

"Come over here Harry" called Angus "They are lining up for the
first race. Quick or you'll miss it.Let's go."

Too late. No going back now. Nothing else for it. Head up, shoulders back, big smile. Get on with it. *Que sera sera!*

Harry joined his pals at the rails and could see that Bungalow and Aris were at the traps ready for the off. Thunder had drawn the third lane. Aris had removed the blanket and remarkably the rotundness of Thunder's middle was not all that noticeable. They might just get away with it.

Harry was feeling a little better. Maybe, just maybe no one would notice with all the activity. The ample Marella slid into place alongside Harry and for a moment Harry did not notice.
"I am here Harry" whispered the ample Marella "To give you some moral support. We must all cheer for Thunder."
"Thank you Marella. Your support is appreciated" said Harry, not believing what he was saying.

The noise and cheering from the crowd was ear splitting. All bets had been laid. The dogs were ready for the off.
As the hare came speeding round, so the dogs were released and off they raced.
"Come on Thunder" screamed the ample Marella, waving her arms and deafening everyone within twenty feet of her. "You can do it."

The dogs approached the first bend and Thunder was doing well in third place. Harry could not believe his eyes. Surely with all that extra weight he could not keep up. But to everyone's amazement keep up he did.

The Luqa supporters were going crazy. Thunder was doing better than anyone had hoped. As they came into the strait, their joy began to wane. Donner had taken the lead. Thunder could not keep up with the pace and started to drop back, fourth, fifth, he was now last as the field crossed the finishing line.

"Oh Harry!" consoled the ample Marella "I am so sorry. He started off so well. Come and have a drink. It will cheer you up."

 "Thank you Marella" said Harry "But I must get down to the kennels and talk with the lads. We have another race to worry about."

"Maybe Lightning will do better Harry" said Andrew "Early days. It can only get better. See you later in the bar."

"Thanks Andrew" said Harry "See you later."

Angus and Idaho had already set off for the kennels and George and Harry sped after them.

"I hope Bungalow put the blanket over Thunder after the race" said Harry still worried that they would be found out.

"It will be OK" reassured George "They know what they have to do."

   As they reached the enclosure where Aris and Bungalow were waiting for them Harry was relieved to see that both dogs had their tartan regalia on.

"Cheer up Harry" said Aris "I think Thunder did very well considering everything."

"Very well! Considering what? He is about a stone overweight. He is not a real greyhound and he clearly has not the stamina for a full race" Harry was distraught.

"Now that's not fair" said Angus "He put up a good show as far as I'm concerned. This was his first competitive race. All he needed was a bit more incentive."

"Like a rocket up his....." added George.

"Not on George. Not on" rebuked Angus "With a bit more trraining and a strricter diet I think we can make him into a good rracer."

"Your faith in the dog is appreciated" said Harry without any conviction "But we have other matters to concentrate on now. What are we going to do with Lightning? The line up will start soon and we haven't got a plan."

"As I said, we could always stick a rocket up...." offered George

"Stop it George" said Harry "We have to take this seriously or this will be the last time we get invited."

"I think I might have a solution" said Idaho.

"Go on" said Harry desperate to try anything.

"Well" Idaho lowered his voice to its conspiratorial level  "Thunder and Lightning are the sons of Fart. Right?"

"So" said Harry.

"Think about it. What is it that motivates Fart more than anything else in the world?"

"Sleep" replied George.

"Well, yes, but what else?"

"Cauliflower" said Bungalow.

"Oh! Come on be serious. But you are getting warmer Bung."

"I would say sausages" offered Aris.

"Right on mate" said Idaho emphatically. "Sausages are the answer."

"How can sausages be the answer?" Harry was confused "It is sausages that have been the problem. That is why they are overweight."

"I will explain" Idaho pulled the conspirators closer.

"If we can attach a sausage, nice and hot and sizzling, to the hare, when Lightning gets a whiff it he will bolt off like a flash of lightning– true to his name."

"That's true" said Aris "Fart was at his motivated best when he thought there was a chance of a sausage. I guess his off–spring will be the same."

"That's all very well but the other dogs will smell the sausage as well" said Harry.

"Yes but they have not been brought up on sausages like Lightning. Their diets have probably not even included meat. Chances are they won't be bothered" said Idaho.

"He has a point" George was warming to the idea.

"OK. Let's say it might work, but how do you fix a sausage to the hare without anyone noticing?" asked Harry.

"Leave that to me" said Idaho. "Angus, Bung and George can create a diversion. Start an argument or something and distract attention away from the hare. Meantime I will strap a hot sausage to it. The organisers will be too busy restoring calm so that they can start the race that they will not notice."

"Mmm" Harry was in deep thought "What if it all goes wrong?"

"We can blame it on some naughty kids" said Idaho "We can say they did it for a joke. Stop worrying Harry. It will be OK. Trust me."

"It's worth a try Harry" said Angus "I say let's do it."

"OK. But on your head be it if it all goes wrong" Harry resigned himself to the plan and in the absence of any other suggestions, what else could he do.

"Bungalow, go to the burger van and buy two hot dogs with the biggest sausages in them" ordered Idaho.

As Bungalow set off, Angus led Lightning towards the starting traps. In what must have been a clear sign of good luck, Lightning had been drawn to trap one. This meant that he would be closest to the hare as it sped past.

"Fate is on our side "remarked Aris. "It is all up to Lightning now." Bungalow returned with the hot dogs stuffed up his tea shirt in the hope that no one would notice.

"Take them out Bung" said George "You are making everyone look at you."

Bungalow sheepishly removed the rolls and gave them to Idaho.

"No, I only want one" he said.

"Then what shall I do with the other one?" asked Bungalow. clearly puzzled by what was going on.

"Give it to Angus."

"To Angus. Why?"

"When Lightning reaches the finishing line he will be expecting to eat a sausage. We can't disappoint him can we?"

"You see Bung" explained Angus "I will grab Lightning, give him the sausage and put his jacket on while you lot make a lot of noise and fuss to divert attention. Idaho will slip off and remove the evidence from the hare and everyone will be happy. No one will know."

"I am getting very nervous about this" said Harry "I hope it does not go wrong."

"Harry" said Idaho" The best thing you can do is go with George to the owner's enclosure and get yourself a stiff drink. Mix with the crowd and act as if everything is normal. Leave everything to us."

"Easier said than done Joe. But I guess you are right. See you all later and good luck" Harry and George left the lads to it. It was crunch time. If Lightning failed to perform like Thunder did then the whole enterprise would have been a fiasco. If anyone realised that the dogs were not what they were supposed to be, then utter disgrace.On the other hand if Idaho's plan worked and Lightning did win, then ...wow!

"Harry, where have you been?" It was the ample Marella complete with a large G&T in her hand "I've been looking all over for you. Come have a drink with Marella."

"Thank you Marella, you are very kind but the race is about to start and I mustn't miss it. My dog, Lightning is running" said Harry ducking out of the offer.

"I know" she replied "Isn't it exciting. I have bet twenty Euro on him. I do hope he wins then we can spend my winnings in the bar together."

"I will look forward to that" Harry suddenly thought that winning the race was not so important anymore!

"Quick Harry, they are lining the dogs up. You mustn't miss this one" called George.

As the dogs were getting ready for the off there was a sudden commotion and raised voices. Clearly some sort of argument had broken out. Angus appeared to be in thick of it. The stewards quickly stepped into the affray to break it up so that the race was not delayed. This was Idaho's chance to attach the sausage to the hare which he did without anyone seeing him.

Standing up he nodded to Angus whose six foot, sixteen stone frame was dominating the fracas. Angus immediately stopped and apologising to all around walked away. The stewards keen to get on with the schedule resumed their positions and started the race.

The hare sped past the line up as the dogs were released. Lightning got the first whiff of the sausage still sizzling from the oven. His ears pricked up, his nostrils widened. Sausages. Sausages. What more incentive could have a dog have than a hot, sizzling sausage. Lightning took off at appropriately lightning speed.  The sausage was his and no one was going to get to it before him. Round the first bend, along the strait, into the second bend down the home strait, Lightning was a good two lengths ahead of Herr Schafer's Blitzen.

The ample Marella was screaming with delight from the enclosure

"Go Lightning, Go Lightning. *Iġri,iġri, iġri* ." She waved her ample arms in the air, her ample proportions flailing bodies to the right and left of her.

Harry could not believe his eyes. Idaho's plan seemed to be working. He had never seen Lightning run this fast. Lightning was his father's son. No doubt about that.

To the ecstatic cheers of the Luqa supporters, Lightning crossed the finishing line well ahead of the next dog. He had done it. The ample Marella embraced a bemused, disbelieving and very emotional Harry. For once he did not complain. Lightning had done it for him.

"He's won. He's won. Lightning has won." Bungalow was shouting at the top of his voice. "We did it. We did it."

"Well actually Lightning did it" said Aris calm as ever.

"Yes mate. But he had a little help from h s friends" said Idaho.

"Now Angus, grab the dog and I will find the hare."

Angus took hold of Lightning and covering him with his tartan overcoat fed the second sausage to a most deserving animal. Idaho calmly stooped down and retrieved the sausage from the hare. Fortunately no one was looking. Why would anyone care about the hare when they had the dogs to celebrate and take care of?

All had gone well. Better than expected. But it was important now to remove the dogs from any prying eyes. Aris and Bungalow quickly loaded the dogs into the back of Aris's Morris Oxford and set off unnoticed for home.

Back at the enclosure Andrew and Marella were looking for Harry to congratulate him and help celebrate the unexpected win. Harry who had managed to extract himself from the ample Marella was doing his level best to disappear before she dragged him to the bar. Too late. Andrew had spotted him.

"Harry. Over here. Let me buy our hero a drink. What will you have?"

"Blue label please" said Harry.

"Blue label! Blue Label! No. No, this calls for a tot of our finest Scotch" said Andrew. "It's not every day that a man's dog wins so magnificently. Two lengths in front they said. Wonderful."

"And I won a nice sum of money from the bookies" added the ample Marella.

"So everyone's happy then" said Harry "I guess we can all drink to that."

To the relief of Harry, they were joined at the bar by Angus and Idaho. Harry took Angus one side.

"Did Aris and Bungalow get the dogs away OK?" he whispered.

"No problem" answered Angus. "All safely despatched. Not a sausage in sight and no-one asking questions."

The relief on Harry's face was a picture.

"Drinks are on me" he said.

"Harry. You are so generous. I'll have a G & T . Heavy on the G, light on the T." Marella was first in line with her order.

"This is a special day for all of us" said Andrew "It has taken ten years but we have seen Harry's dream come to fruition. I am going to make a toast to Harry, to Thunder and Lightning and to the new stadium."

Harry was embarrassed by all the attention but inside he was justly proud of what had been achieved. His inheritance from Aunty Alice and of course Joan's most generous contribution had been essential to the success. But it was really the incredible support that he had had from the villagers of Ħal-Luqa that had made the dream come true.

"Thank you Andrew. And thank you everyone. I would also like to thank Andrew and of course Marella for all their hard work and for their belief in me. And to my dear sister Joan and all the villagers of Ħal-Luqa. Without them none of this would have been possible. Here's to all of you."

Andrew gave a Harry a friendly hug while the ample Marella blew him a kiss and a mischievous wink. As the drinks flowed so the chatter became louder. Everyone was talking about the success of the stadium's first meeting. No one noticed the stewards enter the room.

"Your attention please" A loud voice called for silence.

It was one of the stewards. Harry's heart nearly stopped beating. They have found out! I am going to be exposed! I am going to be humiliated or arrested or banned for life!

"I need to speak with Mr Harry Barber. Is he here, please?"

There was nowhere to hide. Nowhere to go. He had to own up.

"Yes. Over here. I am Harry Barber. What can I do for you?" Harry feared the worst. The game was up. Someone must have found out that his dogs were not the real thing. He would be branded as a cheat.

"Mr. Barber, I have a message from the President of Malta congratulating you on your wonderful achievement and for establishing the new sport of greyhound racing on our island. You, your sister and residents of Ħal-Luqa are invited to the presidential palace for a garden party to celebrate your success."

A great cheer followed this announcement. Harry was stunned. Far from being banished to the dungeons, he was to be feted by the very top of society.

"Congratulations Harry" Andrew was the first to shake his hand."You deserve it". Harry's mind was in a whirl. It was all too much as friends and strangers stepped up to shake his hand and offer their congratulations.

"Just smile and milk it for all you can" whispered George in Harry's ear.

"Congratulations mein freund" Herr Schafer grasped Harry's hand, crunching his fingers in his enthusiasm "A magnificent race. Your Lightning is a fine dog. He will be unbeatable especially if he loses a little weight."

"Thankyou Ludvig" said Harry wondering if Ludvig knew more than he was letting on.

What Harry and his party did not know was that the race stewards had been looking for Harry. As the dogs had been whisked away they had not been able to examine them after the race as regulations required.

"Ah Mr Mayor, Can I trouble you for a moment?" It was one of the stewards.

"Of course" replied Andrew "What can I do for you?"

"We are looking for Mr Barber. We need to ask him some questions" said the official.

"Really. Is it anything I can help with?" Andrew was a shrewd negotiator and guessed something was not quite right.

"Well it is just that his dogs have disappeared and have not been examined after the race as our regulations require."

"I see" said Andrew, now fully convinced that Harry was in trouble. "Perhaps I can help" he said taking the official aside. "Mr Barber is a very good friend of mine and I am sure that he may have misunderstood your requirements. In any case, let me explain to you" the Mayor put his arm around the stewards shoulder and in conspiratorial voice said "I trust that you will understand that none of today's events would have taken place, nor would there have been any dog racing in Malta and you would not have had a job if it hadn't been for Mr Barber. I am sure you realise that for Malta this is a great prestige event and the start of a new industry that will attract many tourists and assist the economy of the island. It would be a shame if a small oversight was blown out of all proportion. Do you get my drift? Perhaps you will not need to talk to Mr Barber after all. Eh!"

It only took the steward a matter of seconds to get the Mayor's drift.

"In the circumstances Mr Mayor, we will let you get back to the celebrations. Thank you for explaining the situation."

Diplomacy at work in Malta and none better at it than the Mayor.
   The party was in full swing. Winners, losers, it did not matter. Everyone had had a great time. The Luqa contingent decided it would be wise to revert to home territory and continue the celebrations at Ho's bar. They paid their respects and farewells to the patrons and jumping into Harry's trusty Chevrolet Impala set off for a triumphant drive to Ħal-Luqa where they would continue their celebrations. Ho had already set the bar out for a celebration of their achievement.
"That was a fantastic day" said Angus "Shall we do it again, Harry?"
"I don't think my nerves would stand it Angus" replied Harry "Anyway you know as well as I do that Lightning never strikes twice!"

# A Sad Day

The morning after the day before! Or to be more precise the evening after. Ho's bar was buzzing with talk about the great day. Everyone had enjoyed their day at the races. Many Euros had been bet on Thunder and Lightning. What they lost on Thunder they recouped on Lightning. Forasmuch as Thunder had let them down Lightning had made up for it. Even Carmena who said betting was the work of the devil had a flutter. She was careful not to tell Pawlu how much she had won of course. That was for her to know and him to wonder. But then he had secretly had a bet as well.

All the talk was about Lightning and how he had sprung from the traps and led the field the entire race. Surely his name will now go down in history as the fastest greyhound in Malta. Toasts to Harry, to Thunder and Lightning, to Angus, Idaho and Bungalow, to Andrew and the ample Marella in fact to everyone and everything that moved resounded round the bar. But then the Ho Chi DO Chi Bar was well known for the regularity of its toasts. And why not? Good people, great friends, always ready to help a fellow villager. That was Ħal Luqa. And now the village was famous. It was only natural that they should have a party to celebrate their success.

No Lights was playing the yellow piano entertaining the patrons with jolly foot tapping tunes from yesteryear. Do had again produced a magnificent feast from nowhere and Ho was pulling pints as fast as he could.

"Hey Bung" called George "Where is Fart? Not like him to miss out on some free food."

"He is asleep in his Villa, I think" answered Bungalow "I will go and get him."

"We should drink a toast to Fart when he comes "whispered George to Harry "After all he is the father of the winning dog."

"Keep your voice down George" Harry glanced around to see if anyone had heard "We have got away with it so far. Don't spoil it. Anyway I am pulling out from any future meetings."

"What!" exclaimed George "Just when you hit on a winner, you want to walk away. You are stark raving mad."

"I have decided I can't stand the strain" said Harry "Joan is OK with it and so is Angus."

"But, but.... I am speechless" said an exasperated George.

"Good let's hope you stay that way" said Harry.

"But what about your investment?" he asked.

"We will keep our shares but we will be sleeping partners. The dogs will not be running" explained Harry.

"You really have thought this through haven't you? Sleeping partners, eh! Just like Fart I suppose."

As he spoke Bungalow re-entered the bar white as a sheet.

"Bung whatever is the matter" called Carmena. Pawlu pulled up a chair for a clearly distressed Bungalow.

"Get him a brandy Ho." called Harry "Make it a double."

"What has happened Bung, old chap" asked Aris.

"It's Fart" the words were almost inaudible "He has gone."

"What do you mean 'gone'?" asked Harry "Shall we send out a search party?"

The bar was as silent as a grave as they realised exactly what Bung meant.

"He's ...." Bung could not get the words out.

"He's left us?" said Carmena softly "You mean he has passed away." Bungalow nodded and broke down in a flood of tears.

 Carmena took him in her arms to console him as everyone stared in stunned silence. Surely it was not true. Fart had always been there. A faithful companion to Bungalow for nearly twenty years. Loved by all even when he dropped one. There were tears in everyone's eyes even the cynical George. It seemed like Fart had been part of village life forever. If he was not sleeping in the magnificent kennel, *Villa tal-Kelb ta Siġġiewi,* that Pawlu had built for him, he would be at the side of his master, Bungalow. His ability to smell a sausage from miles away was renowned and clearly this skill had been passed on to his offspring Lightning much to the appreciation of Harry and all the lucky punters in the village. Fart would be sorely missed.

As the villagers settled down after the initial shock they began exchanging stories of Fart's many escapades. The riotous revelry of the early evening had become solemn.

Bungalow had recovered his composure and was staring into his beer as the villagers tried to comfort him when the Kappillan appeared. News travels fast in the village. He went over to Bungalow.

"I am so sorry to hear of your loss Bungalow" he said "I will help you to pray that he has gone to safe place."

"Thank you Kappillan" mumbled Bungalow "He is my dog so I will bury him properly but if you could give him a blessing I would be very pleased."

"Of course" replied the priest.

"Don't worry Bungalow, George and I will make all the arrangements" said Harry "Just tell us what you want and we will deal with it."

"Thank you Mr Harry and you Mr George" replied Bungalow.

"And I will make you the finest coffin you have ever seen" said Pawlu "leave it to me."

The tears welled up in Bungalow's eyes once more. Fart would have the send off he deserved. No doubt about that. The midnight hour approaching, the bar began to empty as the patrons left deep in thought and in memory of their good friend. Pawlu made straight for his workshop. No time to lose.

Once again he was called upon to honour Fart. He would not let him down. Years ago he had picked up a rather worn but large mahogany table which he had stored in the expectation that it would one day be useful. That day had come. He worked through the night cutting and sawing and polishing so that by daybreak he had made a coffin worthy of such an animal.  He had no doubt that Bungalow would approve.

The funeral was arranged for the next day. As is the custom in most hot countries the burial always takes place within forty eight hours of death. Bungalow had decided that Fart would be buried in the high fields overlooking Wied Iż–Żurrieq. He would find peace there.

The mourners had all gathered at the edge of the field and out of respect they had all worn black. Such was their regard of this remarkable dog that even the Mayor and Mayoress had turned up to pay their respect.

Pawlu opened the back of his pick–up to reveal the coffin. The mourners gasped at its magnificence. It would take four pall bearers to carry it over the rough ground. But Pawlu had already thought about this and so that no one would stumble and drop the casket, he had made two long staves for the bearers to carry it with. It was like the Ark of the Covenant all over again and with just as precious a cargo. Earlier that day Bungalow had found a crevasse high on the garrigue which he had widened enough to accommodate the casket and it was here that Fart would find his final resting place.

The procession was headed by Bungalow who was wearing his uncle's best black suit. He had at his side Lord Nodagan and Her Ladyship both on short leashes lest they saw something move and took off. Following them was Harry and Joan with Thunder and Lightning and the rest of Fart's litter were led by Angus, Idaho, Aris, Pawlu and Mario. Anyone watching would have wondered what was going on. But then this was Malta where anything can happen – and often did.

The sarcophagus was lowered into the grave with great care and reverence. The Kappillan said a prayer and gave the blessing with compassion for the animal that had been part of Luqa village life for nearly two decades.

"I thought the Catholic church said that animals don't go to heaven" said George quietly "Hope the Kappillan does not get struck off."

"No idea" said Harry "But this is Fart. A more human dog I have never seen. The Kappillan knows what he is doing."

Carmena threw a bunch of roses into the grave.

"To make it smell nice" she said "After all it is Fart!"

The mourners discreetly laughed more so when someone threw in the biggest sausage roll you have ever seen.

Amongst the many mourners were six or seven farmers from Siġġiewi who were each carrying a cauliflower. Fart had been brought up on cauliflower. Siġġiewi was where he was born and raised and Siġġiewi is renowned for the quality of its cauliflowers so it was appropriate that he should eat cauliflower. Indeed it has to be acknowledged that the emissions from Fart's rear end for which he was named was due in no small part to his affection for that vegetable.

The farmers tossed their cauliflowers into the open grave as a token of their respect. They made the sign of the cross in due reverence as Bungalow proceeded to fill the grave with rocks and placed a small commemorative plaque at its head which read:

*B'tifkira-għażiża ta'*

*Fart,*

*Il Kelb ta Siġġiewi.*

*Limar jiltaqa' mal-Mulej*

*15 Awissu 2015*

*Mitluf imma mħux minsija*

*Strieħ Fil-Paċi*

Tonio who had brought along his clarinet raised it to his lips and began to play the 'Last Post'. A fitting tribute to Fart who had spotted every 'last post' in the village during his long life. The delicate solemn notes of Tonio's rendition lolled across the garrigue to be absorbed by the patiently waiting sea which was used to drinking in the tears for lost ones.  As Bungalow laid the last rock so he broke down in floods of tears. Carmena and Joan rushed to his side to help him up. It would take a lot to console him.

"Go ahead and cry, *jaħasra*" said Carmena "He was your best friend. Only right you will miss him."

"Come on Bung" said Harry "Let's all go and see Ho and have a last drink in his memory."

The mourners set off for Ħal Luqa and Ho's bar where Do had prepared a fine buffet consisting entirely of sausage rolls. Fart would have been over the moon!

"Over here Bung, old chap" called Aris sliding a large brandy into his hands."Thank you Mr Aris" said Bungalow "I can't believe that he has gone."

"Well maybe it was as well that he went in his sleep" said Carmena trying to comfort her distraught friend "At least he suffered no pain."

"And he has left you a fine legacy, don't you know" said Angus in an attempt to cheer him up.

 "What do you mean?" said Bungalow somewhat puzzled.

"His offspring of course" said Angus "The sons and daughters of Fart. They will be as famous and loved as he was."

Bungalow appeared to cheer up at the thought.

"Angus is right" added Harry "Lightning is already known throughout Malta as the island's fastest greyhound. Lightning, son of Fart."

No sooner had Harry said the words than he realised what he had said. He could have bitten off his tongue.

"Guess the cat is out the bag now" muttered George.

His great secret would now be common knowledge. His deception would be made public. Lightning's name would be removed from the hall of fame. He slumped into his chair totally defeated by his unfortunate revelation.

"What's up Harry?" called Idaho grinning from ear to ear.

"You know what's up you idiot" cried Harry "I've blown it. Everyone now knows that Lord Nodagan did not sire the dogs. It was Fart all along."

"Really" laughed Idaho "Well that is a surpr se. Let me ask all the people of the village about it."

 Idaho addressed the assembled villagers saying

"Hands up all of you who knew who the real father of Her Ladyship's litter was."

To Harry's amazement the entire bar raised their hands and their glasses. Harry could not believe it! They had known all along yet no-one had said a word! *Luqajin* stick together.Their lips were sealed.

"But, but" stuttered Harry "You all knew and you kept quiet. Why did no-one say anything?"

"What and spoil a good thing! Are you joking? The village has never had so much excitement and in any case we are *Ħal Luqajins* we do not grass on our friends" said Pawlu.

"You better believe it Harry. Your secret is safe with us and ever will it remain so. Am I right Luqa?" called Andrew.

"*Iva. Iva. Iva*" chanted the patrons.

"Ok Ok" shouted Harry above the noise "Calm down now. Thank you all for keeping quiet about my secret. I was worried I must say and I appreciate your discretion but you won't have to worry any more as I am withdrawing from the race game and to prove it I want to give you Bungalow the ownership of Thunder and Lightning. Here take their leads. They are yours now" said Harry handing the dogs over to a very happy but somewhat bemused Bungalow "And what is more I am giving you the kennels at Dingli. After all the farm belongs to your father so it is only right."

Bungalow could not believe his ears. Was it really true? He was now the owner of his own kennels!

"Will I still be the Chief of Security?" asked Bungalow.

"Of course" laughed Harry "You can be chief of anything you want. You are the boss now."

"And I can wear my uniform?" he said "Can I keep the car?"

"Bung, it is all yours. Enjoy it. You deserve it" reassured Harry. "You are now a man of substance."

"Then can I please ask a favour?" said Bungalow.

"Name it" replied Harry.

"You have always called me Bungalow and I think I know the reason but in future can you call me by real name?"

"No problem" said Harry a little taken aback. Obviously Bungalow had suffered all these years from his nick name and had never said anything. Although the name had stuck out of fun and with no malice intended it had clearly had a bad effect on the lad "But what is your real name? I don't think I have ever heard it."

"It is Nicholas Camilleri" said Bungalow proudly "And I wish to be called 'Kola'. "

"Everyone" called George standing up and raising his glass "Here's to 'Kola' and his new kennels which I guess he will call the 'Kola Kennels'."

A great cheer rang out. Kola had a grin on his face as wide as any that Ho could muster.

"The rest of the Fart family will go into the care of Angus and Joan, George, Aris and Pawlu. Herr Schafer will adopt Lord Nodagan and Her Ladyship."

"What about you Harry? Aren't you having one?" asked Joan.

"No. Not me, much as I would like to but..." Harry hesitated with a mischievous grin on his face "Well I might as well come clean. You remember all those years ago when we talked about me getting a greyhound?"

"Yes, I remember" said George "It was a choice between getting married and buying a dog wasn't it? You said getting married would be a dog's life so you might as well get a dog."

"That's right" said Harry "Well, I got it wrong. I made the wrong choice."

"What do you mean 'the wrong choice'?" said George dreading the answer.

"Don't tell me" said a visibly shocked Aris "Surely you're not getting ..." He could not finish the sentence.

   The entire bar let out great shrieks of joy. Harry getting married! Unbelievable! Wonderful! Incredible! Fantastic! Everyone rushed to grab Harry's hands to congratulate him. Who would have thought it! After all these years!

George was stunned. He clasped his beer with a vice like grip trying to take it all in. Harry his best mate getting spliced. No, it could not be.

"Hey George" called Aris "Aren't you going to congratulate your old buddy."

George looked up somewhat dazed.

"Of course I am" he stuttered pulling himself together "Bit shocked that's all. Hey Harry, you old devil. You certainly kept that quiet, didn't you?"

"Sorry George" said Harry "No offence mate but with everything that was going on I thought it better to keep it under wraps until things quietened down."

"Well you have certainly stirred them up now" laughed George who was slowly coming to terms with the news "Anyway who is the lucky lady? Why haven't we met her yet?"

"Well actually you all know her and you have done for a long time" said Harry prolonging the answer.

"I knew it all along!" exclaimed George "Marella is divorcing Andrew and getting hitched to you."

The bar erupted into uncontrollable laughter at the thought.

"Sorry Andrew no offence" The Mayor and the ample Marella were laughing the loudest!

"So, come on don't keep us in suspense. Who is she?" called George, still not believing that he had not seen it coming.

"She is my wonderful housekeeper Lucia" announced Harry. Carmena was aghast. She had known Lucia for years and they were good friends but she had no idea that this was on the cards. Clearly the sisterhood of the Great Guisseppa had failed on this occasion.

"Lucia has looked after me for best part of thirty years and we have always got on well together" explained Harry "Now we are both getting on in years it makes sense to move in together and be there for each other as we get older."

The truth was that Lucia lived in a very small two room property in Triq Il–Ġdida and although she kept it immaculately clean, the roof was beginning to leak and the ancient plumbing and electrics were in need of an update.

The cost would be prohibitive whereas Harry's house was too big for him and there was plenty of room for another. But Lucia being a good catholic knew that if she moved in with Harry the tongues would start wagging and her name would be mud. It was Harry who suggested that they get married. They had known each other for nigh on thirty years and had always got on well. Harry had often shared his personal feelings with her and they trusted each other. It was inevitable. But then Harry was not one to rush into things– although waiting thirty years might be considered a little over cautious!

"Come here you old fool" chuckled Joan as she gave Harry a sisterly hug "Best news I've heard in years. My little brother getting married. Who would have thought it? Ho, bring out the champagne. We have some celebrating to do."

The entire bar was buzzing with excitement. The news had spread around the village like wild fire. Harry was part of the village, everyone knew him. He had lived there for over fifty years and with his pals George and Aris had been involved in every aspect of village life. This would be the wedding of the year if not the century.

"So where is Lucia" asked Carmena looking around "She should be here celebrating with us. We want to congratulate her."

"She will be here in a minute" said Harry "Lorretta has gone to fetch her in the Mercedes."

As the patrons waited for the future bride to arrive Do had been hard at work preparing more food for them. What had been a mournful wake for Fart had turned into a happy engagement party for Harry and Lucia. All the sausage rolls had been eaten and it had to be noted that the main recipients of the food had been Fart's own litter. It seems that the desire for sausages was well established in the genes of his offspring.

Harry called Bungalow to one side and quietly said "Bungalow I did not mean to distract from Fart's farewells old Chap, but it sort of just came out."

"No problem Mr Harry" said Bungalow who was busy polishing his cap badge with the sleeve of his granddad's funeral suit. "Fart would be very pleased with your news. He liked Mrs Lucia. She always gave him a lovely big sausage whenever she saw him."

The hooting of Lorretta's horn announced the arrival of Lucia. Everyone turned to greet her as she entered the bar. By nature she was a shy lady and she was not used to so much attention. Harry took her hand and like two young teenagers in love, he guided her like the gentleman he was to a seat in the middle of the bar.

"My dear friends please meet my bride to be Lucia" announced Harry. 'Bride to be' indeed. Harry never thought he would ever use that expression. Having now made his intentions public he was quite overcome with pride and sheer enjoyment that at last he had a made a decision and one that he knew was right.

"Lucia" cried the patrons applauding and raising their glasses. "Congratulations."

"Do you know what you are letting yourself in for?" joked Angus. Lucia was already blushing.

"If I don't know him by now I never will" she laughed.

   Harry had a special place in the hearts of the Luqa villagers. The warmth of feeling for him was clearly evident. Good old Harry. The Kappillan who had been sitting quietly with Alfred the ex constable strolled over to the happy couple.

"So I guess there is no rest for me is there?" he laughed "One minute a burial, now a wedding. What next I wonder? A christening!"

"Oh No!" exclaimed George "Not a load of little Harrys. Please I couldn't take it."

The entire bar was convulsed with laughter at the thought.

   What a day! It had started out in mournful mood with Fart's send off but had finished with Harry and Lucia's exciting news. This would be new era in the life of the village. Something for the villagers to look forward to. But then Luqa was a village that was used to 'new' eras. New eras tended to come along with remarkable regularity in Luqa. As one era ended another began. From the time when Ho and Do arrived and bought Joe's bar from him after the Millennium to this wonderful announcement by Harry, many eras had come and gone.  Village life had been one of constant excitement and change. Some good some not so good. But each event had been taken in their stride.

   But then that is the character of the Maltese. Resilience, survival, the ability to cope. A characteristic inherited from the Knights and the great siege through the generations to the near

annihilation of the island in World War Two. George had put down that ability to survive to one thing – routine.
"Simple as that" said George on one of his rants "Routine. Stick to a routine and you can cope with anything."

When it came to Maltese life then George was spot on. From the church bells at dawn summoning the locals to the first Mass of the day, the collection of the still hot loaf of Maltese bread from the baker, picking up the Times of Malta, a quick chat with the neighbours on the way home, breakfast, wash and  brush up ready for whatever the day had in store.

The ladies would do their washing on Monday even if it was pouring with rain, then off to the market to catch up on the gossip. Sweeping floors, cleaning rooms, making beds, the days shopping.

Routine. It is what has kept Malta strong. It is what has made Luqa a fine place to live in where everyone trusts his neighbour, where they look out for each other, where they share each other's joys and sorrows. Routine gives stability and trust. Break the routine and it is immediately noticed. Action can then be taken. Routine gives a village security, continuity and strength.

No-one appreciated this better than Harry. He had no time for the modern materialistic life style of the new younger generations. A simple life, that is all he wanted.

Of course the word 'simple' has many interpretations. It can mean stupid, uneducated and naive. But it also means straightforward, no complications, easy to understand and that is all Harry ever wanted from life.

The entire village now hoped that was exactly what he would have with his fiancé, Lucia. A convenient continuation of his routine albeit with a wife!

As Ho rang the bar bell to call an end to the day, so every villager set off with a spring in their rather wobbly steps, hearts filled with happiness, set for a good night's sleep in readiness for whatever tomorrow may bring, just as it had been since time immemorial.

As it was in the beginning, is now and ever shall be.